Calling All Angels

Calling All Angels

A Guardian Angel Chronicles Romance

Barbara Ankrum

TULE
PUBLISHING

ISBN: 978-1-957748-25-2

Dedication

To my parents who inspired this one. Miss you both so.
And to my sweet David for all your love and relentless belief
in me. This one's for you, my love.

Chapter One

E MMA JAMES'S GRANDMOTHER had once told her that memories, like dreams, were as fluid as water. Some swirled up unbidden, like the tide rushing in. Others got pulled out like a riptide—tumbling, secretive, and eventually far away.

But some memories, she said, survive everything. Even death.

But let's face it, Gran was a little crazy. Or in Emma's mother's words, a little *woo-woo*. Gran was a free spirit soul. Her best friends were people who believed in things like soul circles and past lives. All the topics that drove Emma's pragmatic father nuts when she sat with them around their dinner table, talking her "nonsense." They wouldn't argue, but before long, her father would politely—but pointedly— change the subject. Eventually, she stopped talking about things like that with them, but in Emma, she had a captive audience of one. Whether winding yarn around dreamcatchers together, studying cloud formations, or hunting for healing crystal geodes, her grandmother did her best to counteract her parents' eyebrow raising.

1

"Your parents are doing the best they can," her grandmother had whispered in seven-year-old Emma's ear as she kissed her goodbye the last time she ever saw her. "But all they know is what they know. Nothing more. There is a whole world out there you can't even see, Emmalyn."

Emma had adored her and humored her, though when she was grown, she'd ultimately sided with her father on the *woo-woo* stuff. Even though, true to her word, Emma's late grandmother would swirl up in her memories at odd times, gently nudging her to look again. Reminding her that, indeed, some memories survived even death. Because during the worst of Emma's breakups, her many failures, and even her wildest successes, there her grandma would be, rushing up in her memory.

Now as Emma stood in the rain on that dark, grassy bank above the shallow ravine, watching the EMTs work to extract that poor woman from her overturned car at the bottom, she felt her grandmother beside her, whispering in her ear to remember this moment. That it was important.

Maybe, Emma decided, this was one of those moments she'd like the sea to take with its riptides and undertows. She didn't want to remember the loneliness of this place or imagine what that woman's family would soon be going through.

Emma wanted to forget the grinding sound of the car's wheels spinning in the air and the sight of the deep ruts cut in the wet, grassy bank that slashed through the headlights of the ambulance parked nearby, the smell of fuel littering the grassy shoulder of the road.

She wondered who had called 911. Probably one of the other drivers who'd stopped, like her, standing a few feet away.

Was the woman alive?

Oh, she hoped so.

As the EMTs began to pull the woman out, Emma caught glimpses of the woman's hair, a similar auburn color and shoulder-length like Emma's own. There was blood. *Poor thing.*

"Get a collar on her," she heard one of them say.

"Do we have a pulse?"

"Thready. BP's seventy over forty," another replied, half under his breath. "We're going to lose her if we don't get her stabilized now."

A hollow feeling hit the pit of her stomach. That didn't sound good. Strange that she could hear their voices so plainly, even as she stood watching like an idiot, a good fifty feet away in the shin-deep wet grass on the bank.

She should offer to help. Hold that woman's hand. Call her family for her. *Something.* But of course, the EMTs had this handled. Getting in the middle would only put her in the way.

No, she should walk back to her car. Get out of this drizzle. Drive away. Put this awful memory behind her. After all, she couldn't even tell them what happened. She hadn't actually seen the accident that had sent that woman over the edge.

No, no. She'd arrived after the fact. Now there was nothing she could do here but be a spectator.

But—she turned to look at the road, at the debris scattered across it, the deep scar of tracks leading over the edge—where *was* her car?

Parked on the road were only the EMT vehicles, the fire truck, and two other cars—not hers. Their drivers—men, strangers—stood overlooking the bank as well. They were speaking together in hushed tones.

"…guy spooked as soon as I stopped. I didn't get a good look at him—it was so dark. He was trying to help her, I think. But he took off," the younger one in the gray hoodie told the other, a man in his sixties with a paunchy belly. "I asked him if he'd called 911, but he said he didn't have a phone on him. Said he couldn't wait. Just took off. So, I called. They got here quick."

"Man," the other one said. "That's cold. Good thing you stopped."

"Yeah, people are weird in a crisis." The man in the hoodie still had blood on his hands. He bent down to wipe them off in the wet grass. "I did what I could, but…"

"Might have saved that woman's life. If she makes it. These guys know what they're doing," the older one answered. "My brother-in-law was a paramedic. He…"

The man droned on, but Emma stopped listening as she

searched the dark road with increasing worry. Her car was…*nowhere*.

Silly. Of course it was here…*somewhere*. She was always losing something. Her keys, her purse. Her peace of mind. The car must've been parked behind the fire truck, she supposed. Walking in that direction, she moved past the two men who were still deep in conversation about the woman below. They didn't seem to notice her or make any attempt to include her in their discussion, which was fine with her, really. That seemed gruesome. Instead, she focused on the feel of the rain-slick grass slapping at her ankles as the EMT workers lifted the woman out of her car onto a backboard. *Don't look,* she told herself. *You don't want to remember this.*

When she got to the other side of the fire truck, her car was nowhere to be seen.

Emma rubbed her damp, aching temples. This evening was turning into a nightmare. She'd misplaced her car, and now she was going to be late for her meeting with—she frowned, the name momentarily eluding her—with…*right*…with Dan Gainer, the real-estate investor she and her niece, Aubrey, had been wooing for months about the Bayside penthouse property. A meeting she was last-minute taking for Aubrey who had a surprise dinner with Jacob's parents, who were in town.

Emma reached for her phone. *Oh no.* Her phone was in her purse. Apparently, she'd left that, along with her brain, inside her missing car.

Starting to feel panicky, she spun back toward the two men watching the EMTs carry the woman up the hill. "Excuse me," she called to them. "Excuse me. Can you help me? I seem to have misplaced my—"

"Yeah, this road has always been bad," the older guy was saying to Sweatshirt Hoodie Guy. "My wife has appealed to the city for some streetlights out on this road, but nothin'. Claimed it was too rural. Wasn't it just last month that motorcyclist ate it on this curve? Such a shame."

"I'm sorry," Emma began again, "I don't mean to interrupt, but—"

"Tell me about it," said the younger one. "I like motorcycles as much as the next guy, but you won't catch me out here at night on one."

Emma pressed her lips together and walked up practically between them. "*Excuse* me. I-I seem to have misplaced my car."

"Even a car won't protect you out here," said the one with the paunchy belly. He nodded toward the EMTs carrying the woman up the hill. "Oh, look. Here they come. I suppose we should give 'em our names. In case she makes it. Jeez Louise. Looks bad."

"I don't think you should count her out just yet, do you?" Emma said, feeling a little indignant at being ignored. At least she hoped the woman would be—

"What kind of car is that anyway?" Paunch asked. "A Lexus SUV?"

Emma blinked. She turned her attention back to the battered, upside-down car. *Her* car was a Lexus SUV.

"Hard to tell," Hoodie mused. "It's so messed up, but yeah. Might be."

Cold seeped into her. Glancing down at her feet, she noticed one of her shoes was missing. She curled her bare toes into the muddy grass.

Okay, stop it now. This is just getting weird.

Something more than simple curiosity drew her haltingly toward the woman on the backboard the EMTs had struggled up the hill with and were now carrying across the road. Emma still couldn't get a good look at her, circled as she was by emergency workers. Except for the glimpse of her right hand, the glint of silver on her fourth finger.

A simple silver band exactly like Emma's own ring.

She froze. Her thoughts tilted. *Wait. No.*

That can't be right. But—

"Looks like her name is…uh…Emma. Emma James," said the EMT holding a wallet. *Her* wallet. From *her* purse as the others moved toward the ambulance.

Emma sucked in a breath. *No.* She squeezed her eyes shut. *No, no, no. This can't be happening!*

"Emma, can you hear me?" the female EMT asked, leaning over that other Emma. The one that wasn't her.

"I can hear you! I'm Emma. I can hear you. I'm right here!" she practically shouted.

"Her pulse is—"

"Charge the defib."

A strange whining sound cranked inside her head. *Wait! This is all wrong. Am I—? I-Is she—?*

"Charging!"

No. I don't have time for this. My life is too full, too busy! We're leaving first thing in the morning for Turks and Caicos. The whole team. This is ridiculous—

"Stay with us, Emma," implored another as they loaded the other Emma onto the ambulance.

Wake up, Emma. Wake up! This is all a bad dream. Just wake up!

Water dripped off her nose as she jerked a look to her right, to the men still standing on the bank shaking their heads as they spoke to the police officer about the accident. And to the left where two firemen tidied the ropes they'd used in the rescue.

Alone as she'd ever been, there in the dark, she spun around to suddenly find another man—one she hadn't seen before—watching her. *Seeing* her with something close to astonishment. He looked vaguely familiar, like some figure out of a film she'd once seen, but the memory blinked away as soon as he met her eyes. He took a tentative step in her direction, looking nothing like the others, who were all business and urgency, but quite separate from all that. She couldn't make out why. Except for the fact that his odd clothing… Black leather pants, knee-high boots, and loose linen shirt—did not fit here. Just as she didn't fit.

He shook his head, confused, taking one more step in

her direction, his voice a hoarse, familiar if disbelieving whisper. "Violet?"

Emma blinked as something like lightning scored through her—a memory, a flash of something searingly hot and far away.

Then, everything went black.

"YE SHOULD'A WARNED me it was her," he growled, staring at the woman lying on the ICU bed across the hall. "'Twas wrong of you, Marguerite. You know it."

"*Je suis désolé,* Connor? Who exactly?"

Marguerite Ciel, Connor's erstwhile mentor and overall pain in his arse, feigning innocence at his question with her Cajun charm, would be amusing if it wasn't so predictable. Over the last few centuries, she'd had her hand in every turn of his development as a guardian. But mostly she'd thrown doors in front of him disguised as walls. Most of those doors had opened peacefully. With this one, however, she'd gone too far. Clearly, she knew it.

"Violet," he answered. "*My* Violet." No, not his—ever actually—but at least a woman who was the image of her.

Corralling her small, fluffy dog, Enoch, Marguerite lifted him into her arms and tucked him against her, possibly as protection from Connor's wrath. Glancing toward the bed that held the woman from the accident last night, she replied, "I believe her name is Emma. Emma James—"

"Ye know it's her as well as I do. Or some twenty-first century version of her."

"You know it's her because…?"

"Because I'd know her in the dark," he snapped. "I'd know her in any century or on any continent. Whether we understood each other or not. I'd know her."

"Ah." Marguerite sniffed. "Your point is…?"

"My point is ye had no business pairin' me up wi' her when you know my feelin's on the subject." He stalked past her down the hospital corridor of St. Elias, contemplating all the ways in which walking away from this assignment—as he should, by rights, do—would burn his chances for the Council seat he'd been eying for longer than he cared to recall. Not that he gave a flyin' flock about that now. Not when he'd found himself face-to-face with Violet again. Whether she remembered him or not wasn't important. Though, for the briefest of moments out there in the dark last night, he imaged she had.

Marguerite was tight on his heels. "Roland approved the assignment. How was I to know Violet—or who this Emma person once was—was still such a *peekon* in your side?"

A thorn, indeed, that still poked him under his skin after all these years. Marguerite knew full well, of course, his feelings about Violet. If this was some kind of test, then he was bound to fail it. Because he wouldna be paired up with the likes of that woman again. Even if it was merely to escort her home, deposit her at the Gates, and bid her a fare-thee-well.

"As a third degree," he argued, "I shouldn't have to—"

"You'll have to take that up with Roland, you know," she interrupted, knowing Connor would get nowhere with the senior head of the Council. Roland was fair but famously unmovable when it came to changing his mind.

He rubbed a hand across his mouth. "Aye, I'll do that. Then I'll take a sharp stick to the eye. Just to prove I enjoy losin'."

Enoch barked in his direction, a yippie little sound that Connor interpreted as opinionated. He narrowed a glare at the little dog. "Did I ask for your thoughts on the matter?"

"Roland's not all that bad," Marguerite pointed out, peering over Connor's shoulder at the woman. "Why, look what happened with Elspeth Aloysius."

Elspeth. Elle. A guardian/friend several ranks below him who had recently taken matters into her own hands and gone against every rule Roland had set up for her. Connor had to admit, he admired her for that. He secretly envied her outcome. But on this matter, he felt certain that if Roland had deemed it so, there would be no recourse. Even when he'd gotten the assignment, there had been a crimson flag of urgency attached to it. To turn it down could only hurt him in his quest for a Council seat.

"Fine," he bit out. "I'll escort her. But I'm not doin' a lick more than is required of me. Don't expect me to do orientation or take her through first steps at intake."

She pressed a finger to her lips and glanced toward Emma's room, where she lay surrounded by beeping machines and tubes. "Bein' sure of yourself has always been one of your greatest strengths. But also one of your basic weaknesses, Connor. Who said her outcome is already determined?"

Not determined? "Isn't it? Don't play with me, Marguerite. We know each other too well."

"This is no game, Connor. Our path—our job—as guardians is as deep as the bayou is wide. It's filled with things that'll either eat or sustain you. You get to choose which."

A sigh welled up from inside him. "I know I'm in trouble when you begin talkin' in metaphors."

A smile eased the serious expression on her face. "'Twas you who said you wanted that seat on the Council, no? Do this, I can pretty much guarantee you will get what you need, Boo. *C'est' tout.* It's time for me to go. Be seein' you soon, eh?"

"But wait!" he said. "What about—?"

Too late. She was gone.

Frustrated, Connor glanced down at the glowing dial on his inner wrist. A clock, of sorts, that measured not time but instead the completion of intention. It was a senior guardian tool, one he knew intimately.

His dial read -4 percent. He gave his wrist a few unproductive taps with his finger, then sucked a sigh through his teeth. Never before had he had a negative reading of completion on his wrist dial. If the thing wasn't broken—which was technically impossible—that could only mean he was somehow losing ground in getting Emma where she needed to go, instead of making headway. With a 100 percent completion rating required for this job to be signed off by Marguerite, clearly, this was already going badly.

Stubborn woman. But that was no surprise. Emma James—or whoever she was—had better hurry it up and get her head around her situation. Because he had better things to do than sit around waiting for her to—

He whirled at the touch of someone's hand on his arm to find *her* standing beside him, her wide-eyed gaze every bit as shocked as his own.

"Oh!" Emma cried hoarsely, pulling her hand away as if he'd burned her. "You—you *are* real. I mean—" She stared down at her fingers, flexing them in a testing sort of way. "You can *see* me. Right?"

Violet's voice with a twenty-first century inflection.
Balls.

"Aye," he bit out. "I can." To him, her spirit looked every bit as corporeal as he himself did. Even though he wasn't, in fact, corporeal at all, as evidenced by the nurse who had just walked right between the two of them.

Shocked, Emma stared down at herself. "Am I…*dead*, then?"

"Not exactly."

"Then what is *this*?" She gestured at the transmutability of her body, at him. At this other place they occupied.

This, Connor decided, was apparently Hell.

Because, just as he had the night before, he was momentarily incapable of pulling his gaze from the familiarity of her mouth or reconcile the effect the sound of her voice had on him or quit remembering the feel of Violet's cheek against the backs of his fingers. In spirit, she bore none of the bruises or abrasions her body had suffered in the crash. Except she was minus one shoe, of course, and her auburn hair was a bit of a mess.

Which, to his chagrin, only hardened her appeal.

Oh, aye, he would have words for Roland the next time he saw him for forcing him into this—

Looking suddenly paler than pale, she reached out again, her fingers gripping his forearm, as if he could somehow keep her from falling, which she looked in very real danger of doing. He stiffened at her touch.

"I feel so…odd," she said.

"Ye willna faint," he told her. "It's only the adjustment that yer feelin'."

Her eyes were suddenly shiny with tears as she released her grip on him and backed against a wall. "The adjustment to…what?"

Still transfixed by this apparition from a long-ago life, Connor hesitated. He could almost remember when she was the one he could count on. Trust, even.

"Adjustment to what?" she repeated.

"To the in-between," he said, hardening himself to the stricken look in her eyes.

"In between…what exactly?"

"That world," he explained slowly, indicating her body in the bed, "and the next."

"Oh!" she cried. "I *am* dead!"

"Calm yerself. Yer not dead. Yet. Nor are ye quite all there on the other side, either."

"Don't tell me to calm myself! Hasn't anyone ever told you that's the wrong thing to say to a woman in a moment of crisis?"

"Not precisely, no."

She squeezed her eyes shut, concentrating. "Okay." The spitting image of Violet nodded unconvincingly. "And so…you're also in this…in-between?"

"No. I've definitely chosen sides."

Her gaze slid over him, taking in every inch of his features. "I…I don't understand."

"Ye will."

Suspicion clouded her expression. "And…who are you?"

"Name's Connor." He watched her closely to see if his name sparked any memories. It did not seem to.

"Connor," she repeated, testing the sound of it on her tongue. "I'm Emma."

"I know who ye are." He just stared at the hand she'd extended until she dropped it back to her side.

"Something tells me I don't want to know how you know that." Rubbing her temples, she squeezed her eyes shut again. "However, maybe you can tell me how I get back to my side of things?" She gestured at her body in the bed.

"I canna help ye there. Sorry."

She tilted a look at him, then slowly nodded. "Ahhh. Of course you can't. Because everybody knows you never really solve problems in dreams."

This revelation seemed to both relieve and excite her. She paced around the small room. The dream explanation was all too common among these mortals, who rarely accepted their fate when the time came. Sometimes, it took weeks. Denial was powerful. Connor folded his arms.

"I mean…" she continued, "in dreams, you just go round and round until you finally figure it out by some kind of…magical realization what the whole point is of seeing yourself lying in that bed looking like…*that*. I mean, maybe I've been working too hard lately or…it's like that awful one where I've overslept for a college exam and I've actually forgotten to go to class for the whole semester? Or…or maybe it was that *Law of Attraction* podcast I listened to that messed my sleep up for months last year coming back to bite me again, considering"—she waved a finger at him—"you. Here. Looking…like that. Hot, actually." She blushed a little. "See? That's something I would never say in real life. Alas, you're not real. In dreams nothing gets resolved and then you wake up. Voilà!"

Amused, or oddly flattered, he narrowed a look at her.

"Yes. So, I'm going to wake up now. Goodbye, cute Scottish dream guy. *Connor.* Nothing personal." She bowed slightly at the waist to him before she squeezed her eyes shut, trying to wake up. She spent a good thirty seconds at it.

But when she opened her eyes, nothing had changed.

"Wake up, Emma," she told herself, slapping her cheek. Then again, harder. "Wake up." Out of one eye, she peeked to see Connor still staring, his jaw cocked.

"It's okay," she said. "It's just more like a nightmare."

"You dinna recall the accident?" Connor reminded. "Wi' your automobile?"

Emma frowned at him. "That was part of this dream. I think."

"I'm sorry t' say 'tis no dream, Emma."

"Okay, just stop it now. I'm just gonna—" She paced around from the foot of the bed, climbing down atop herself to align herself precisely with her body. "It's probably just logistical." Squeezing her eyes shut, she winced with the effort to make something happen, but of course, nothing did. Nothing at all. The monitors attached to her body kept right on beeping, albeit at a more erratic pace. But not a finger or an eyelash moved.

He folded his arms, leaning back against the wall. "Go on, then."

She lifted her head, scanning her still comatose body. "When I want something, I…I make it happen."

Absently, he glanced at his wrist again. The dial read -5 percent. *Och. This is going in the wrong direction.*

"I'm sorry," she said, looking up at him. "Am I keeping you from something important?"

"Matter of fact," he mumbled but didn't finish the thought aloud.

She sent him an offended look just as the nurse whose name tag read *Katrina* spun through the room, checking the IV and beeping machines beside her body.

"There you go," Katrina soothed. "That'll make you more comfortable now."

"No! I'm not comfortable at all!" Emma practically shouted, sitting up. "I'm right here! I just need to wake up. Can you help me? I'm dreaming. I can't seem to…" Waving her hand at the nurse, it passed right through the other woman without notice. Emma shook her hand. "Oh. This is bad." Sitting up, she scooted off the edge of the bed. "Very bad."

"They canna see us. Either of us," he told her.

"Okay," she said finally. "Okay, just for argument's sake, let's say you're right. I'm not dreaming and I'm in this…this in-between but you're…*not*. So, what are *you*? Some kind of"—she swallowed thickly—"ghost?"

He shook his head, restraining a laugh.

Eyeing his clothes, she ventured, "Time traveler?"

He frowned with a look down at his apparel.

"*Angel?*"

He gave her a pistol-point with his index finger. "Guardian, more accurately."

Again, she narrowed a look at him, apparently gauging his veracity. "*My* guardian, I suppose you're going to tell me?"

"Technicality," he said, gritting his teeth. "It's a temporary assignment."

"Oh. I see. Well. To be perfectly honest, I...don't really believe in any of that stuff. Angels—sorry, *guardians*. Crop circles and all that."

"Is that right?"

"Uh-huh. Or ghosts even. My gran did, but she was a little...you know." She whirled a finger around her temple. "I believe that nonsense is just people trying to justify—"

"Their complicated existence?"

"Yes. *No.* Trying to...I don't know...hope. That's all."

"Hope, is it?" he said. "And ye don't? Hope?"

Glancing about the room, she replied, "Is that a trick question?"

"The Scots say: *Were it not for hope the heart would break.*"

"My heart," she pointed out, "is none of your business."

"And you not believin' what's happenin' does make this whole situation a bit of a dilemma for ye now, does it not?"

"Maybe." She moved around the room, trailing a finger along the surfaces of the machines, though, again, not exactly touching them. "Anyway, I can't quite recall how it all—the accident… How it—"

"Happened? That's irrelevant, isn't it, at this point?"

"*Irrelevant?*"

"Aye. 'Tis of no matter now how but where ye go from here."

"Maybe to you it's irrelevant. But it's not to me. I mean, look at me. I'm…I'm *invisible*. How did that accident happen? Why, for heaven's sake? I'm a good driver. The best driver."

"I meant irrelevant in the sense that the crash happened. Now you're here. With me. In the in-between. See how that works?" He didn't mean to mock her exactly. But speaking to Violet brought out the worst in him.

She considered him. "You're a bit cranky as guardian angels go, aren't you? I mean, in the traditional sense."

He cocked his jaw. "I'm only here to facilitate."

"Okay, I'll play along. Facilitate what, exactly? My…death?"

"Most likely."

"Wait…" She stopped with a puzzled look. "Wait. In my dream, I saw you before, didn't I? Back on the road? In the dark. You called me by some other name."

Slowly, he unfolded his arms, scowling at her.

"What was it again? Velvet? Veronica?"

He ground his teeth together.

"No. *Violet.* That was it. You called me Violet. Didn't you?"

"No." He couldn't meet her eye now. "Maybe. That's no' important."

"I think perhaps it is. Maybe that's the key to my dream. Who is this Violet person?"

"Nobody."

"Hmmm." She eyed him for a full ten seconds before she walked closer to him, coming practically under his nose. She gave a sniff as if she were testing out his scent, scanning the full length of him from the ground up until her gaze landed on his face.

He felt the rake of her gaze rush through him like the heat of a flame.

"I thought angels couldn't lie."

"And I thought you didn't believe in angels."

Emma tapped her steepled fingertips together thoughtfully. "Show me your wings."

A bark of laughter escaped him. "What? Why?"

"To prove to me you are who you say you are. You could be anyone. You could be—" She pointed downward. "Why should I trust you? I mean, how do I know you're here in my best interests?"

Connor glanced around the ICU, where medical personnel flitted in and out of the sliding glass-doored rooms past desperately ill patients, most of whom had their own stoic guardians posted nearby, a mixture of males and females. The constant sounds of the place were like the thrum of a hundred high-pitched drums, all disjointed and struggling.

21

Even Emma James's heart. "If I do show you, then what?"

"Then"—she swallowed thickly—"I-I don't know."

"Then, you'll stop arguin' wi' me?"

"Maybe."

He was much taller than she was. He loomed over her until she was forced, by his mere will, to take a step back, bumping into the bed before rounding it to the other side. She lifted her chin in direct defiance of his most practiced intimidating look. *Whatever resolves this unpleasant reunion in the quickest way possible.*

What compelled him, no doubt, was pride. Ego, even. Because he'd never shown his wings to any mortal before. But she wasn't mortal, was she? Not exactly. So, in one effortless movement, he unfolded and stretched his wings.

Chapter Two

H IS WINGS TOWERED over him magnificently—if he did say so himself—translucent, brilliantly etched against the green hospital walls, a feathery show as much a part of him as his breath or the memories that inhabited his skin.

Their full effect elicited a gasp from Emma as she stumbled away from him, colliding with the wall behind her, sliding down hard onto the bare linoleum floor, against the wall, with both hands over her mouth.

Against his better judgment, he settled his wings back into place where he should have kept them all along and crouched down beside her. No doubt the Council would use this bit of pride against him in his review. "Believe me now?"

She waved a silent hand at him, at an apparently uncharacteristic loss for words.

Was she…*crying*?

Balls.

He steeled himself against her tears. He'd never been any good with a woman's tears, least of all hers. He coached himself against feeling anything at all. *Dangerous, dangerous ground, Connor.*

"Dinna cry," he told her, but it came out more like a demand than a comfort.

"Don't tell me what to do." She gulped back a sob. "I think I'm entitled. Don't you?"

"'Tis no' like you."

"How would you know what I'm like?" She blurted out the question on a sob. "And this is all a little much for me. This is all some kind of mistake. I'm not ready to die, though I'd hardly expect you to understand."

He sank down beside her on the floor. "'Tis my job, after all."

She sniffed. "You're not very good at it, though, are you?"

That stung. He was good. Very good at his job. Just not with coming face-to-face with Violet here in the in-between. Not Violet exactly, he reminded himself. Just her doppelgänger.

"And look," she said, a fresh sob pulling at her voice. "I've even lost my shoe."

Someone slid the glass door to her room open. She sat up, wiping her face with the heels of her palms. "Aubrey!" she cried, jumping to her half-shod feet.

The young woman at the door only had eyes for the woman lying in the bed, who was poked with tubes and breathing apparatus. With a thick bandage around her head, and a swollen eye, Emma looked nothing like herself. Aubrey's eyes were red—from crying, he supposed. She clutched a tissue in one hand as if it would somehow save her from the wave about to crash over her at the sight of Emma in the bed.

The nurse standing beside her took her arm. "It's always a shock at first to see someone you care about like this."

Aubrey nodded. Tearfully she made her way beside Emma's bed. "Can I...will I hurt her if I touch her?"

"No. Of course not. We've got her heavily sedated."

"Sedated?" Emma shot a look at Connor, who was getting to his feet. "Well, that explains everything! That's why I'm so fuzzy. Right?"

He sent her a rigid look, unwilling to say what she might not be ready to hear.

The nurse went on. "But she may even be able to hear you if you talk to her. At least, we think so. Sometimes."

"Yes. Yes. I can," Emma cried. "Thank God you're here, Aubrey. I'm right here. Look at me!" But of course, Aubrey didn't.

Connor stepped back, curious about this girl.

"You're her only family, then?" the nurse asked the girl, adjusting the drip on Emma's IV.

Aubrey nodded. "She's my aunt. I mean, she's only ten years older than me. My mom was her older sister. But my parents both passed. It was just the two of us left. Emma's taken care of me since I was sixteen."

"Oh, dear. I'm so sorry," the nurse said. "We'll all keep a good thought for her. We'll do everything we can." The nurse pressed a hand against her shoulder. "Five minutes, now." She quietly left the room.

Emma pressed her knuckles against her lips, watching her niece. Against his will, Connor felt a little sorry for Emma as she began to realize he'd been telling her the truth.

"Oh, Em," Aubrey whispered, gently holding Emma's still hand above the covers. "This can't be happening. I can't do this alone. I need you to be here. I need you. The doctors say you have a chance. A good chance, okay? But please, Emma. You've got to fight. This can't be how it ends for you. For us."

Emma made an effort to gather herself. "I'm *not* dreaming. Am I?"

Connor lifted one brow but said nothing.

With tears in her eyes, her niece shook her head and stared up at the machine beeping away above her bed. "I can't lose you, too. It can't be your time. You're just on the brink of…of everything, Emma. If you go, who will walk me down the aisle? Who will kiss my children? You. You have to. Please. Emma. Please try."

Emma teared up, too. She touched Aubrey's shoulder. "This is all wrong. I promised to stay with you always. I never expected—" She heaved a shuddering breath. "I'm going to clear up this mistake, Aub. You'll see." She stared up at Connor.

"Everyone's outside in the waiting room," Aubrey told her. "They've been here all night. We're all so worried for you. I love you, Em."

Moved by her words, Emma watched her niece for a long time. "I love you, too. Why don't we say those things to each other more? I didn't say it enough to her. I should've told her every day."

"She'll be alone if…?" Connor began. It wasn't his job to worry about such things, but curiosity bested him.

Emma nodded. "Except for Jacob. Her boyfriend. But they're…he's…they're just dating. She's like my own daughter. A daughter I'll probably never have. Now."

Feeling empathy for Emma—Violet—was something he hadn't anticipated. Nor did he welcome it, even now. But once, a long time ago, he himself had longed for a child. A child with Violet, a little girl with depthless brown eyes and her mother's strength. But that was never to be for him, either. Violet had gone on to give that traitor, Sykes, children, a fact that had torn at him for longer than he cared to admit.

But he'd let all that go.

No, he hadn't.

Aubrey squeezed Emma's hand as the nurse popped her head back in the door. "There are some police officers out here who would like a word with you, Ms. Wilhelm."

"With me?"

"They're waiting outside."

Emma shot Connor a questioning look. *Police?*

He glanced at his wrist again: -6 percent now? *Oh, for the love of all that's—*

Aubrey patted Emma's hand, then left with the nurse.

"I'm going with her," Emma told him, starting to follow her niece.

"Don't," he warned.

"Why not?"

"Because." He indicated her body on the bed, clarifying, as if it was obvious.

"No. I'm walking outside that door now."

"Ye canna." He narrowed his best intimidating look at her. He didn't have the patience for games like—

She took a small, testing step toward the door, watching for his reaction.

Then another.

"Listen to me—"

She took another, reaching the threshold of the doorway, then lifted her shoulders in a *who's going to stop me—you?* gesture.

"Emma—" he warned.

If she scared easily, she certainly didn't show it. Not a bit. Instead, she deliberately placed her bare toe on the other side of the doorway. When nothing dire happened, her mouth quirked in a victorious grin.

Stubborn as a bairn bent on testing her limits.

Once she'd crossed a foot over that imaginary boundary he'd drawn, it was clear there'd be no stopping her.

Connor scowled as she disappeared into the corridor to

listen in on her niece's conversation. *Headstrong, obstinate, perverse.* Just a few of the words that came to his mind as he watched her hover over her niece's shoulder in the hallway as the girl conversed with the two officers in blue. But then, *disloyal* had always been a favorite of his when it came to her. Although he supposed he didn't have the supporting evidence for that word yet as it applied to Emma James.

She wasn't Violet, he reminded himself. Not exactly anyway. Except in all the ways that counted: the way she looked, the touch of sadness in her eyes, the way his body reacted to her…

He did his best to avert his gaze from the woman lying in the bed, hooked up to machines. Surprisingly, but for a few cuts and abrasions, her poor broken left leg elevated in a sling, and the nasty bruise around her eye, she looked like the Violet he remembered—a paler, more docile version of the Emma in the hallway.

How often had he found himself mentally rewriting the last days of their history together or composing what he might have said to her if he'd had half the chance? A thousand times, he reckoned. Now was his opportunity to say it to her face. But this woman, this Emma had no memory of him. No soul memory at least. That would come later.

Now she was hovering somewhere between worlds, trying desperately to stay in this one as the other beckoned her, with him as her erstwhile traffic cop, pointing her toward the path of least resistance.

With a final look at the woman on the bed, he followed Emma into the hallway.

"THERE'S EVIDENCE THAT there was another vehicle involved in the crash," the officer was telling Aubrey as Emma appeared at her shoulder. "From the looks of the crash scene, Ms. James—"

"Wilhelm. My name. It's Aubrey Wilhelm. My aunt's last name is James."

He wrote that down in his little book. "So, we've determined that an encounter took place over approximately sixty feet of road."

Emma staggered back a step and leaned against a wall, something niggling at her memory.

"*What?* What...exactly do you mean, an encounter?" Aubrey asked as her boyfriend, Jacob, moved beside her, putting an arm around her shoulder.

"We're trying to connect some debris found on the road with your aunt's car accident. Also the piece of debris found on the scene."

"What kind of debris?" Jacob asked.

"Some parts of another car's bumper. Pieces of a headlight. Some impact paint scrapes on the rear fender of your aunt's vehicle. It could have been a simple hit-and-run or something more intentional."

Aghast, Aubrey said, "You think that someone hit her on purpose?"

Emma turned a stunned look back at Connor, watching the scene from the doorway to her room. He looked quickly away. His indolent lean against the hallway door held no answers and did nothing to distract her from the kick of unwelcome attraction she felt toward him. There was no denying his beauty. Aristocratic yet raw. Honestly, his mouth alone was enough to cause her to break out in a sweat, with that full lower lip always bent in a sexy scowl. A disapproving, sexy scowl. Why was it that she was always attracted to men who judged her? He certainly made no secret of it even as he attempted to seem unconcerned with her plight. He seemed anxious for her to get on with it. Whatever "it" was.

But there was something else. Something in his gaze when she caught him studying her. Something she couldn't quite identify, yet vaguely familiar. Or perhaps it was just the feeling that she found familiar.

Men.

Even male angels confounded her. And that she'd even just *thought* the word *angels* was enough to make her feel like she was losing it. Where was Gran when she needed her?

"Is there any reason you know of that someone might want to harm your aunt?" the officer asked Aubrey, opening his small flip notebook.

"No. Why would they? Everyone loves her."

Her words sent a warm feeling rushing through her. Her

friends, the women who worked for her, were her family. Her only family outside of Aubrey.

"Husbands? Ex-husbands? Boyfriends?" the officer asked. Emma's thoughts raced in a new direction. "Disgruntled employees? Ms. James owns a successful real-estate company, is that right?"

"Yes, she owns it. She built it from the ground up. All of her employees are friends. Women, mostly. Women who needed jobs. Even I'm interning there this summer. And no, she's not married. She's never been married. She was—*is*—pretty much married to her job."

Heat rose to Emma's face. *Married to my job? Is that what she thinks?*

"There was a guy she was dating," Aubrey continued, "sort of half seriously for a year or so. But he's out of the picture now."

"Happen to know his name?"

"Drake. Drake Lasserman."

Drake would never—

"He's a lawyer," Aubrey went on. "Works at the law firm Billford, Bradley, and Cutler. But," she said, "it couldn't be him."

The cop narrowed a dubious look at her. "You sound pretty certain."

"It was over. He knew that. She made that clear."

"I never liked that guy," Jacob muttered.

"Why's that?" the officer asked.

Jacob made a face. "Some guys you just know. They'd sucker punch you when they got the chance or step on you on their way up. That's Drake Lasserman in a nutshell. I've seen him in action in the courtroom." He shook his head.

Sadly, Emma had to agree. Drake was a jerk. Why had she even dated him? What was wrong with her that she always picked the wrong men?

"You a lawyer, too?" the officer asked Jacob.

"Yeah," he said, extending his hand to the officer. "Jacob Warner."

Jacob had never voiced his opinion about Drake to her, but she knew that Aubrey hadn't ever liked Drake. She'd made that pretty clear early on. Despite her youth, Aubrey had seen coming what Emma hadn't much sooner. But Drake wanted control. Emma wasn't about to let anyone control her.

Connor lifted one dark eyebrow as if he'd been privy to that thought. She ignored him.

"My aunt broke it off with Drake weeks ago," Aubrey continued. "It was her idea, not his, but I heard he took it well. As well as one could, I suppose, when it's not your idea."

"Why did she break it off?" he asked.

"That's personal," Emma announced to no one.

But Aubrey said, "Emma said she felt…suffocated. She's a bit of a free spirit, I guess."

Or a commitment-phobe. Aware of Connor's perusal,

Emma bit her lip and looked away.

"Can you think of anyone else?"

"Maybe you should be looking at that debris on the road before you go accusing the people in Emma's life," Aubrey told the officer. "I can't imagine anyone wanting to hurt her."

As a list of potential suspects spun through Emma's mind, a sick feeling swelled up in her. This was her life they were talking about. Her life. Or what used to be her life. But no one she loved would want her dead. It had to be a simple case of road rage. Or a hit-and-run accident.

Emma couldn't seem to quite catch her breath. She felt the hallway closing in on her.

"I just…I can't—" she told Connor before fleeing down the hallway. Away from Aubrey and Jacob. Most of all, from that maddening man who was apparently an angel.

She rushed down the hallway but found herself in the waiting area, filled with people she knew. There were Dierdre, Joanne, Amanda and her sweet husband, Joe. Mark Wallace, who had just joined her team. Even Kinsey Adler, her assistant, was there.

The sight of all of them here caught her by surprise. All of them waiting to see if she would live or die. Amanda was crying. So was Dierdre. Kinsey, her short, boyish hair cut looking uncharacteristically messy today, sat ten chairs over from everyone else looking very…stoic. But Emma couldn't fault her for that. That was just Kinsey. But she'd brought flowers for Emma. They sat wilting on the chair beside her. That was unexpected. Surprisingly sweet of her.

Emma suddenly recalled the conversation they'd had just the other day, when Kinsey had told her she'd earned her real-estate license and wanted to move away from contracts to become an agent. To Emma's regret, she'd tried to dissuade her. Success in her line of work was relationship-based, but Kinsey was not a people person. At all. But now Emma wished she'd encouraged her instead. Good office managers were hard to find, true. But why stand in the way of someone wanting to grow? Maybe she'd surprise everyone.

There was Diedre, who had just gone through a messy divorce, with two young boys to care for, who must have moved heaven and earth to arrange care for her boys to be here. Dierdre was one of her top sellers, but only during school hours when someone else could take care of her boys. It made things tricky for her, but Emma had supported her in every way she could. Still, had she done enough? Had she been too wrapped up in her own career to really notice how much she was struggling?

Even Amanda—a woman who seemed totally together— had to work hard balancing selling condos with juggling her three kids' sports schedules. Joe was fortunately supportive of her work. But sometimes, even the flexible hours were a challenge due to his demanding railroad job.

Looking at that roomful of coworkers gathered together, it struck her not for the first time that, except for these friendships and Aubrey, her life was relatively unfettered by intimate relationships. She had no children to show for her thirty-three years, no husband, and not even a dog who required walking. Just Winston, a very independent, self-sufficient cat. Which said pretty much everything that needed to be said about the possibly "late" Emma James's life. Wildly connection free. Unencumbered by mad love.

"And what about Aubrey?" Amanda whispered to her husband. "Emma is the only family she has left in the world. She'll be lost if…"

"Jacob will watch out for her," Joe told her, patting her shoulder. "He seems like a good guy."

"Three months, Joe. That's how long they've been together, according to Emma. That's not even long enough to know how someone likes his coffee. Much less become family."

Emma had to agree. She liked Jacob. But really, who could actually deserve her Aubrey? She was special, not just because Emma had spent the last seven years as her surrogate "mom." But because from the moment she'd been born, Emma had adored that child. Before she'd started her own firm, Emma had even flown to Rome four times to visit after Lizzy and Daniel had moved there when Aubrey turned seven. Later, when they'd moved back and were off scouting locations for dives, it was Emma they called to stay with Aubrey. Sometimes their trips would last for weeks at a time. It had been one of those times when Aubrey had been with her that her parents had disappeared, never to return.

A pain of that memory was still as sharp today.

She was Lizzy's mini me. Even now she looked so much like her with her thick, dark hair and brown eyes. Never once did Emma forget the responsibility she had to Lizzy and Daniel to see Aubrey through to a happy life without them. Aubrey was likely the only child she'd ever raise. At thirty-three, Emma's prospects of finding someone to father a child for her seemed as…well, as unlikely as her chances right now of waking up—considering there was already an angel waiting for her to go.

She wanted out of this place. Now.

She reached the hospital entrance before she could make sense of her journey there but stopped at the glass front doors.

Somehow, without even fully willing herself to do so, she found herself outside. In the fresh air. Standing beneath one of the dozens of pine trees that lined the parking lot. How had she done that? Frankly, she didn't care because now she felt free.

How strange, being outside in the world away from all that beeping noise of the machines and the sterile smell of the place.

The sound of the breeze sifting through the tops of the trees above was unusually acute, as if she were part of the treetops themselves. Her vision was suddenly sharper, the colors more defined or even exaggerated, as if each color carried its own sound, the green and blue louder than the rest. Even the scent of the pine straw beneath her feet seemed headier, more aromatic than she remembered it. It was as if all her senses had suddenly come alive in this in-between place.

A strikingly colored blue jay stared down at her from a branch above her head. He squawked at her, ruffling his feathers, his beady black eyes focused intently on her.

"Hey. Can you...*see* me?" she asked. The bird ruffled its feathers, then bolted off the branch in a flutter of wings, disappearing into the nearby trees. "I will take that as a yes."

How odd this all was. How terribly odd. She felt strangely helpless. That was not a feeling she liked or was used to. She'd spent most of the last decade of her life pushing herself to survive and, more importantly, to succeed. On most people's terms, she supposed, she had succeeded, building a great company, a crew of friends/employees whose lives were better for that work. Friends who would do anything for her.

By most standards, she was a success.

Just not by hers.

"Yer bein' a wee bit hard on yourself, aren't ye?"

She swung around to find Connor sitting beneath the tree behind her, one wrist slung over his bent knee. Looking...well...looking for all the world like he should be biting into a forbidden apple. With a snake slithering down from above.

"Apparently," she said. "I can't escape you, then."

"Not really. No."

"Did…did you just actually hear what I was thinking?"

"Might've," he allowed, but it was clear he had.

"Well, stop that."

He stared off at the horizon, where the smog from the city had settled like a brownish mantle. "I'm not all that interested, truth be told."

"Oh. Good."

"Fine," he said but nonetheless started following her across the parking lot toward the field beyond as she walked away from him.

Finally, she swung around on him again. "Don't follow me."

"Afraid I must," he replied. "Guardian thing."

She scowled at him. "Keep back, then."

With a slight bow, he answered, "As you wish."

"Thank you," she muttered, adding, "*Farm Boy*" under her breath as she stalked across the grassy field to the sound of his amusement.

"Farm Boy?" he repeated, following some ten feet behind her. "I assure you, I was never a farm—"

She whirled back and he skidded to a stop a few feet behind her. "That was pure sarcasm and a film reference. But rest assured, you're no Westley."

"Westley…?" he asked with an all–too–Westley-ish grin.

"*Princess Bride*?" she said, as if he should know. "Buttercup's one true love? He was brave. Strong. Loyal," she pointed out. "And helpful. Nothing like you apparently."

"Ye've made that determination already, have ye?"

"Obviously. You'd clearly rather be anywhere than here with me. In my darkest hour," she added dramatically. "I'm not even sure why you're hanging around."

"Some of us honor our commitments," he said half under his breath.

"What is that supposed to mean?"

His gaze passed over her like a wave of heat, and he glanced at his wrist again. "We should be gettin' back."

"Go on, then," she said. "Unless I'm about to wake up. Is that why you keep looking at that glowing thing on your wrist?"

"That's not for me to say."

He was the most frustrating man. Angel. *Whatever.* "I'd like to speak to your supervisor."

His laugh made his face change entirely. It made him almost...human. "My supervisor, eh?"

"Yes, please."

"Okay. Well, let me just do a wee check to see if she's available. Nae, she's not. Ye'll just have to make do with me, I'm afraid."

No doubt he'd used that disarming grin of his to charm the myriad of women (angelic or otherwise) that men like him always had flitting around him. But it wouldn't work on her. "Your supervisor is female?"

"Ye might call her a supervisor. But she's not at my beck

and call, ye see."

She lifted a pained look up at him through her lashes.

"What? Don't believe me?"

"You don't seem the type to take orders from any woman."

"And ye say so, why?"

"You may be an angel, but you're still a man."

Threading his fingers together, he propped his hands atop his head, scanning the surrounding field. "Ye never had a problem with that before," he muttered, mostly to himself.

"Before…what? Have we met somewhere before? Pray tell. What have I done to offend you?"

For a long beat, he stared at her. She could almost see an argument going on in his head about how much to say.

"Not you, exactly," he admitted. "But you. Exactly. And *offend* is a mild word."

He was making her head hurt. "Well, riddle me this, Farm Boy. How could I not know you and know you at the same time? Are you being intentionally obtuse? Because I have no idea what you're talking about."

He seemed to have expected as much. "I canna blame ye for that." A muscle in his jaw worked. "I'm goin' back. Comin'?"

He didn't wait for her to answer, simply stalked back toward the hospital doors. As much as he confounded her, as much as she was starting to truly despise him, she couldn't help but be affected by the figure he cut walking through the long grass: his linen shirt clinging to his strong arms and back. The way her breath caught watching the breeze ruffled his too long dark hair.

Stop it!

What in the world was happening to her?

For a long moment, Emma wondered what would happen if she tried to navigate this whole situation by herself. It would not go well, she suspected. She might even die by default. He was her only tether to possibility. But he was as much a mystery to her as this place was, as what had happened on that road last night. However, alone, she would be lost. Adrift in the unknown. Yet to do nothing...to stay locked in the hospital beside her helpless body and leave all the questions unanswered about her accident, about Aubrey's future, about...well, everything seemed unthinkable. It just wasn't in her DNA.

Had someone tried to drive her off the road intentionally? Was it road rage or accidental? Had she simply been distracted? Had she lost control? What was the debris that officer had talked about? She couldn't remember anything about the accident at all. It was as if her memory had been wiped clean.

Even more urgently, something niggled at her. Something important she knew she'd forgotten. Something she'd needed to do. For the life of her, she couldn't remember what.

Emma almost laughed at the irony of that phrase. *For the*

life of her. What if that road had meant the end of that life for her? What if she never woke up? What if Connor was just biding his time, waiting until she…until she died to be rid of her? Were all angels as unpleasant as him? It wasn't her imagination that he seemed to be keeping something from her. No, three times he'd said something he refused to explain. And who was Violet? Why did he seem to dislike her so? More importantly, what had Emma herself ever done to him?

Obviously, nothing. Except possibly ogle him a bit more than strictly necessary. Because, for heaven sakes, the man was—she had trouble forming the word in her mind—*gorgeous.* But aside from the fact that he wasn't even mortal, he was not her type: arrogant, cranky, and full of himself.

So, technically, her type.

Not that any of that mattered at all. But the answers to all those questions felt out of reach.

One thing she knew: If she wanted his help, she would need to change tactics. She would need to get him on her side.

"MY CAT," EMMA announced, appearing at the doorway to her hospital room.

Connor, who'd been standing beside her bed, studying the temporary cast wrapped around her leg, squinted at her now from beneath lowered brows. His intention was to intimidate her, but she showed no sign of being cowed. "Your cat?" he repeated.

"Winston. He's been alone since…all this. I have to go home. You need to help me get me there."

"We've been over this—"

"Yeah," she said. "That might fly if I hadn't already been outside the hospital, a thousand feet away. But here I am. And…there I am. Nothing went haywire. I think you're just making it up that it's dangerous for me to be separated from my body."

"Do ye now?"

"Yes."

"Are ye always this much trouble, Emma?"

She lifted her chin. "Absolutely."

Might've known. Once a troubled soul, always a troubled soul. Connor slouched down into the chair beside her bed, slinging one knee over the armrest. "And what exactly do ye think you'll do once you get to your place? Ye canna feed the wee cat. Ye know that, right?"

"But you can."

"Beg your pardon?"

She knelt beside his chair, folding her hands prayerfully atop his knee in a most disconcerting way. Or, rather, her hands atop his knee had the most disconcerting effect on him. "You can be seen if you want. You said so. You can be physical if the situation calls for—"

He practically snorted. "Not for a cat."

"For Winston you can. He's very special. He—"

"I'm allergic."

Her lips parted with a look of incredulity. "No, you're not."

"Aye, I am."

"You're not even human," she pointed out. "That's impossible."

Not even—? Blast the woman! He rolled to his feet to pace the perimeter of the small room. "You're right. I'm not. Allergic."

She frowned. "Then why not?"

"Just…*no*," he snapped.

She studied him for a full ten seconds with a perplexed expression before a grin appeared on her lips. "No," she said. "Wait. You're not afraid of cats, are you?"

He pulled a face, then turned away from her. "I am not."

"You *are*."

He spun to find her colliding into him, but he caught her by the arms to set her away from him. "No, I am not."

Emma bit her cheek to contain her smile. "Prove it."

Oh, he was going to have a talk with Roland about this assignment, all right, and sooner rather than later. But before she could accuse him of anything else, he took her by the arm and transported her to the stoop of her front porch.

Off-balance, Emma swayed beside him and blinked hard as if trying to clear the dizziness from her head. She glanced up at her front door, then at the street behind them, then pressed her fingers to her temples. "How…how did you do that?"

"Never mind," he said. "You're here. Let's get on wi' it."

Emma stared at the door. "How good are you at picking locks?"

He gave her a condescending look. In the next instant, they were inside, standing in the foyer—staring at the contents of every drawer, shelf, and table strewn all over the floor of her living room. Every piece of furniture was upended or torn open. Every cupboard emptied. Every picture frame smashed and shattered on the floor.

Chapter Three

EMMA STARED AT her home, wide-eyed. Speechless. For once.

"Fair to assume," he murmured, "yer no' just a messy housekeeper?"

Her eyes, when they met his, were brimming with shocked tears. She could only shake her head.

Stepping over the chaos, he lifted a wooden dining chair back onto its feet, out of her way as she staggered into the room, looking at what was left of her furniture.

"Who did this?" she whispered, picking her way through the detritus. She reached for a fallen picture frame—a photo of her and Aubrey—but her hand passed right through it. Her gaze frantically met his. "Who would do this to my house?"

Connor scanned the destruction. "Someone who's not fond o' cats?"

"Winston!" she shouted, moving through the house and taking in the absolute destruction. "Here, kitty, kitty! Here, baby!"

Connor followed her, a wary eye on suspicious corners

where a cat might hide. He wasn't scared of the buggers. He just didn't like them.

But Emma's question couldn't be ignored. Who would do this to her? Or drive her off the road? Someone wanting something from her? Looking for something, clearly. Had they found it? Were they connected somehow to the accident she'd had? He didn't believe in coincidence, so…likely. But what could they want from Emma, a woman with no obvious enemies but a roomful of friends in the waiting room, praying for her recovery?

Chances were the cat wouldn't see or hear her calling him out. Only certain animals could. But he wouldn't convince her of that.

"You live here alone?" he asked her. "Except for the cat, I mean."

"No. Aubrey is staying with me for the summer. Only until she gets a place of her own. Her idea, not mine. I'd let her stay with me forever. She just graduated college. This place was fine when I left yesterday evening. This must have happened after Aubrey heard about my accident, after she went to the hospital. Thank God she wasn't here, or—"

Or she might've been caught up in whatever was going on with Emma as well, he thought. It was not just this room that was tossed. Every room in her house had been gone through with sledgehammer precision.

After looking in every corner of the house, Emma stood in the middle of the living room, staring at the chaos.

Overwhelmed seemed too poor a word to describe her state. *Despairing* seemed more accurate. Because not only had her life been imperiled by what had occurred last night but now, it seemed, her niece's life might be as well. Whoever had broken into her place had spared no violence in their utter destruction here. As if to leave a message to her. With an effort, he reined in his impulse to comfort her. He couldn't allow himself to care about this woman. She was a job, nothing more.

"Can ye see anything missing?" he asked her.

"My cat," she answered. "I can't find Winston."

"Maybe he got out when whoever did this came in. The wee buggers always find a way. Nine lives and all that."

"He's never been out a day in his life. He wouldn't." She bit her lip. "Do you think they took him?"

Not if they valued their lives.

The cat was her one true possession, he surmised, the thing she valued most after Aubrey. Violet, too, had been an animal lover. She'd been mad for the mare he'd gifted her when they'd gotten engaged—a pretty, dapple gray she'd named Easter for the nearby Easterlin Valley she'd loved so well. Even now, he could recall the tender care she'd taken with the mare and the animal's devotion to her in return. The horse followed her around like a pet dog. He could still remember her sparkling laughter at his gentle ribbing that she'd ruined a fine hunting animal with such tenderness. How ironic that such a woman could so easily betray the man whose heart she'd held in her hand, as she had him.

Connor slammed his eyes shut to gather himself, pushing away the memory of her. He had no will to dredge up Violet in his mind any more than he wanted to feel sorry for this version of her standing before him now. Emma might've been a different woman than the woman he'd once loved, but her soul was the same. If, instead of becoming a guardian, he'd returned for another go at the world, no doubt he would have stumbled into her circle once more as a mortal. Because this wasn't the first time since that long ago life that he'd encountered her in the intervening centuries. But if he had his way, it would certainly be the last.

Distracting himself, he looked under a table beside the sliding glass door, which was open a crack. "Anything else obvious they took?"

She shook her head, rubbing the heel of her palm against her damp cheek. "Everything's here. Electronics"—her television was upside down on the floor; a cracked-screen iPad was lying nearby—"photos. Even my jewelry, which is mostly worthless to anyone but me." The entire contents of her jewelry box were scattered across the kitchen floor.

A half-dozen artifacts from long ago civilizations were scattered across the floor in various states of brokenness. "These were my sister's. All of them from places she'd lived. They were all we had left of her."

She knelt down beside a broken picture frame of a photo of her and Aubrey. She brushed her fingers against the

CALLING ALL ANGELS

cracked glass. "I don't have anything anyone could possibly want. I don't understand. What is happening?"

"We should go back," he said, hardly tempering the sternness in his voice. "There's nothing ye can do here now."

"Back? *No.* I have to find Winston."

"Cats are cunning. They can fend for themselves. Leave out a bit of food, and he'll find it when he's ready."

Her expression sank. "I can't. You know I can't do that. My hands pass right through things. You do it. I'll show you where the cat food is."

Bossy, this one. Fair enough. If that would get her out of here and on to what needed doing. He followed her to the kitchen, where she spotted the plastic container of cat food lying on its side beneath the table.

The skill of materializing was one he'd managed early on and often used in his interactions with the mortal world. Blending in was simple enough, and he did it without ever drawing attention to himself. It was often useful in his job— a faculty his mentor, Marguerite, had perfected long before him. It was she who'd taught him the value of being seen. Of interacting with the mortal world when necessary. As he reached for the food, he reminded himself that Marguerite would answer for this assignment as well, putting him in the path of—

The feline banshee-like yowl struck him only a heartbeat before ten sharp talons sank into his back. He yelped as pain rifled through him. He arched with surprise, tossing the offending cat off his back, landing it in the corner of the kitchen with an almost comical scramble against the tile floor. It crouched there with a hissing growl in the corner, sending a dagger-filled stare at him as Emma dropped to her knees beside it.

"Winston! There you are! Oh, did he hurt you, baby?"

"Did *I* hurt *him*?" Connor blurted, clutching his wounded shoulder. "Aye, right!"

The little hellraiser instantly mellowed at the sight of his mistress, curious but not terrified by her new form. "You frightened him, appearing the way you did," she accused.

"Did I? I thought ye asked me to feed the wee monster."

"The poor thing is half scared out of his mind already with all those"—now she descended into baby talk with the cat—"awful, awful people who terrified you, didn't they my poor, sweet little boy?"

Winston yowled loudly at him again, warning him off, and Connor glared back before undoing the top of the plastic container and tossing a handful of dry food onto the floor for him. Winston pounced on the kibble, all the while eyeing Connor with suspicion.

"I feed him in a bowl," Emma pointed out.

"I didna think it mattered, bein' as all the bowls themselves are already scattered t' kingdom come."

"Please give him a little more. A lot more. Who knows when I'll be back?"

Connor grudgingly obliged, setting down a bowl of water, too.

"I want you to teach me how to do what we did," she said. "Getting here. That *Star Trek* teleporting thing."

"No."

"Why not?"

He slapped the lid back on the cat food. "If ye need to travel, you'll be goin' with me."

"Why is that fair?"

"No one said anything about fair."

She blinked at him. "Fine. Then take me to the place where the accident happened."

"Why?"

"I need to see it myself. I need to remember."

"Because?"

"Don't be belligerent."

His jaw worked. "Why do you need to go?"

She reached out to Winston, who meowed plaintively at her. "There's something I'm forgetting. It's important. We'll be back in plenty of time for the...other me to wake up. Once they pull back on the drugs, you'll see. This was all a big mistake." The cat stared up at her. "I'll be back, Winston. All of me will be back soon, you'll see. Don't be scared."

Unexpectedly, Winston rubbed up against Connor's leg before he sat, curling his extravagant gray tail around himself under the kitchen chair.

"See?" she told Connor, who was exploring the painful

divots in his shoulder with his free hand. "He likes you."

"Oh, is that what this is?" he said with a snort of disbelief. "Let's go, then, before he changes his mind again."

"Wait." She turned back to the living room. "First, I want to know. Why am I here?"

"In your *living room*?" he asked as if he were speaking to a dim-witted Labrador retriever.

"No. I know what we're doing *here*. But why am I…here with you? Like this?"

Surreptitiously, he glanced at his wrist again. Now it was at +2 percent. *Huh.* With a frown, he lifted his gaze back to her. "Every case is different," he told her. "But *this* never happens unless it's close."

"It…meaning death?"

He wouldn't meet her gaze, but he nodded.

"Are you keeping the truth from me because you don't like me?"

"My feelin's have naught to do with anythin'. I've been assigned to ye. T' help ye muddle through this part. And so ye know, 'twas not my decision. Though even guardians generally get a choice in the matter."

Her expression flattened. "Your choice would not have been me, is that what you're saying?"

He looked back at Winston, who was still eating kibble off the floor. "T' be honest, no."

Color rose to her pale cheeks. "Dare I ask why not?"

"'Tis no matter to ye now."

"I beg to differ. I think I have a right to know why you hate me."

"I dinna hate ye." *Exactly.*

"Have I already done something to offend you? Is it my missing shoe? Shoeless women offend you? Or maybe it was my driving skills. Or lack thereof. By the way, I wasn't drinking. I was perfectly sober. I remember that much. I would never... But we've hardly known each other a hot minute. I can't think what I could have done to—"

"*You* did nothing."

"Then why—?" He was clearly frustrating her. "Are you just generally ill-tempered? Because that seems antithetical to everything angels are supposed to be about."

This woman. She did amuse him against his will. He contained his smile, though. No point rubbing salt in the wound. "I suppose I am."

"But there's more. Isn't there?"

Silence stretched between them, broken only by the sound of kibble crunching and Winston's soft growls as he ate. "We...might've known one another once."

Taken aback, she said, "Known each other? I don't recall, and I think I would remember you. In fact, there's no doubt in my mind. Was it before you became...this?" She gestured at his angel form with her finger.

"'Twas a long time ago," he admitted, but even that went way outside his sharing boundaries.

"How long ago?"

"We should go if it's the accident scene you're wantin' to see."

"No, no," she said. "You started this. Now you have to tell me."

"I don't actually. And I'd rather not get into it."

She blinked at him, her mind still apparently scanning her hard drive to remember him. There was a flicker of something, he thought, but it was unlikely she'd have a passing glance at such a memory, even in her state of being. He had no desire to dredge up old wounds with her. It would only cause both of them pain. And that wasn't his job. No matter what, it wasn't what he'd been sent to do. He started for the door, but she wasn't about to go so easily.

"Do you know why I'm so good at my job?" she asked him, still standing in the middle of the room when he looked back. Her chin was stubbornly up. The look in her eye was more pity than anger. "I sell things. Real estate. Homes. Lifestyles. I find a property to pair up with the person who belongs with it. Almost anyone can do a halfway decent job at selling real estate. But to excel, to build a company that people put their trust into, one must be able to read people, to get underneath their skin, see past the thing they say they want. To discover the thing they actually need. Understand what they're not telling me."

He didn't like where this was going.

"I can separate myself from my feelings about a person, whether I like them or not, because that's my job. You?

You're not the type to suffer fools or hide your feelings or even, maybe, let go of a grudge."

Connor just stared at her, giving nothing away.

"But I," she continued, "have nothing to do with that old grudge, whatever it is. I'll remind you that I am the one out swimming in the deep water here. And that you're the only thing I have to hang on to. So, I'm asking you to put aside whatever that is and help me. Can you do that?"

"Aye. I said I would. Let's get on wi' it." As long as it would help her move on.

"FYI. I'm appealing the decision." She pointed upward. "I just want to be clear."

"Whatever." She could talk a big game, but in the end, it wouldn't be her decision. And for the record, he didn't appreciate noticing the way the light settled across the soft curve of her cheek and glimmered in her eyes. He especially resented the way his body reacted to the sight—in direct opposition to the very thing he needed most: to be rid of her. But sensations were brewing inside him out of nowhere, distracting him from his bitterness. He frowned. His *business*.

"Fine," she practically chirped.

"Fine," he replied. He opened the door with a look back at the cat, who had slunk into the living room behind them. "Sit," he told him. "Stay."

Winston found that ray of sunshine to stretch out in, licking his dinner from his lips.

"See you later, Winston." Emma walked over and held

out her hand to Connor. Reluctantly, he slipped his fingers between hers, threading their hands together.

He sucked in a breath at the touch, the feel of her hand in his. He felt the shock of it again all the way through him, like a bolt of energy. Connection energy. Energy as familiar to him as the sound of his name coming from her lips. Pulling away, taking control with his hand on her arm seemed prudent, but he didn't. He simply allowed her hand to stay in his, and he took her where she'd said she wanted to go.

DURING THE DAYTIME, the road looked nothing like the it did at night. There was nothing sinister about it aside from the tire tracks that disappeared over the edge just past a curve in the road. There were no cars going past here now. Only a few cows grazing in a nearby pasture, staring across the road, chewing their cud. Emma wondered if they'd witnessed what had happened last night. If they'd heard the sound. Could they see her now? Could they see Connor?

She didn't know why it mattered, but it seemed if someone, anyone could see her, she was still in the game. She still existed.

Beyond that hill on the other side of the road lay the town of Schooner's Bay and the Pacific Ocean, with its steep cliffs and rock formations stretching out from the shoreline.

She'd loved that beach growing up—the sounds, the smells of it. She'd spent many afternoons with her friends, prowling its sandy stretches or hiking atop the high cliffs at the edge of the forest. But she hadn't done that in forever.

She'd had her first kiss on those cliffs. With Aaron Pleasure. She smiled, recalling his name. He'd been teased mercilessly for it, but he wore his name proudly. His kisses introduced her to a whole world of adolescent pleasure. Afternoons, they would hike along the cliffside trails and he would identify conifer cones for her from all the different trees. He'd point out the seabirds she'd never noticed before. He knew all their names, where they nested, or how far they'd flown across the world to be there. She'd been impressed by all his nerdy knowledge, attracted to his dimples, among other things. But most of all, he'd drawn her into a world outside her own small one, peopled by her dysfunctional parents who'd been, at the time, going through a divorce. She'd even coerced her older sister, Lizzy, along on one of their hikes that summer when she was on a break from law school. Lizzy and Aaron had talked the whole way about sunken treasure in the shipwrecks off the coast. It would be the first but not the last time Emma had heard about Lizzy's obsession with the sea. Lizzy would later marry her long-time boyfriend, Daniel, give up the law, and they would spend the rest of their too-short lives hunting treasure far away from her.

And Aaron? Her first kiss, possibly her first love, would

move away at the end of that summer, and she would never see him again.

Funny how things worked out.

One by one, all of those people she cared about would disappear. Pass away. Her parents, on separate coasts; Lizzy and Daniel, halfway around the world. Everyone except Aubrey.

Lately, her life had become a rush from one day to the next, a blur of business meetings, phone calls, and contracts. At night, she would fall into bed late—alone—and it would take her hours to get to sleep. The irony that now she couldn't seem to wake up didn't escape her. Maybe it was payback for all the stress.

And vacations? Vacations had become merely rewards for her employees. Not relaxing for her, as she'd wanted them to be perfect for everyone. She worked hard to make them perfect, scheduling every last detail to make the women who worked for her feel appreciated. But who appreciated her? Why did she never take time for herself as well?

She'd been afraid of dying for a long time. Irrationally afraid when she allowed herself to contemplate such things. She couldn't say why. Maybe because she'd long ago stopped believing in those things her gran believed. In things like angels or crop circles or believing in dreams.

Now here she was, walking with an angel. *Her* angel. Contemplating the place that had taken her out.

Below, her car had been towed away. The ground was

gouged and torn up where it had landed. The memory of watching the EMTs pull her out rushed over her. She sat down hard on the sun-warmed hillside, feeling shaky.

Connor turned back to her. "What?"

"Nothing," she said, rubbing her temples. "A little PTSD is all."

"PTS—?"

"It's like déjà vu. Only physical."

He nodded though she thought he didn't know what she meant at all. "Sometimes," he said, "it's for yer own sake that ye canna recall. Sometimes we take ye out before."

"Before impact?"

"Aye. 'Tis a mercy sometimes."

"Is that what happened to me?"

"'Twasn't me. Marguerite, I suppose, had her hand in it."

"Marguerite?"

Connor glanced around as if half expecting her to appear. "Ye asked about my supervisor once. That would be her."

"But I saw you there last night."

"After," he conceded. "Time travels in a different lane there. It's no' like here where everything follows an orderly line. Time hardly matters where I'm from."

"Is that why you keep looking at that dial on your wrist?"

Stuffing his hand into his pocket, he looked away toward the scene of the accident. "I thought you wanted to look around."

He wasn't about to tell her anything personal. Anything that meant anything to him. Emma gritted her teeth and got to her feet. Well, two could play that game. She started down the hill, slipping a little on the dew-slick grass with her one still-bare foot. Maybe she'd find her shoe around here somewhere. That seemed the least she could do.

At the bottom of the hill, heaviness pressed on her as she scanned the ground. There were bits and pieces of her car still scattered around, but the scene had already been gone over by the police, as evidenced by the little orange flags poking out of the ground where they'd found items of interest. She broadened her scope, walking much farther away from where her car had landed, not even sure what she was looking for. She spotted something glinting in the sun in the long grass. It was hers. A tall, gold, crystal-studded thermal cup with her agency slogan inscribed on the front.

Emma James Realty—When What You're Looking for Is Home

Apparently, the police hadn't done a stellar investigation here. What else had they missed?

The cup was dented now, broken, and more than a few of the rhinestones had been knocked off. She'd loved that cup. But looking at it now, lying alone in the middle of this grassy slope, it seemed…embarrassing. Unnecessary. She was suddenly glad the police had missed it. Why had she put rhinestones on a thermal cup anyway?

She couldn't pick it up, so she left it where it was.

Connor was walking across the way, brushing aside grass with the toe of his boot. Every now and then, their eyes would meet across the field and she would quickly look away. Even now she felt him watching her as if he were trying to figure her out. Or musing on that secret he seemed to be keeping about her. Something about their past history? Which didn't make any sense to her.

It was none of her business what had him so bent about her. But his attitude wasn't irrelevant. Not only because they were stuck together until this situation resolved but because she depended on him to help her now that she was stuck here somewhere between her life and…death.

That thought sent a shiver through her. Who could have imagined that she'd be here today, picking through the remnants of an accident that had nearly—maybe—stolen her life? Just yesterday, everything had been going so well. She'd had her life under control, with big deals in the offing. She'd had Aubrey home with her again after being gone for so long at school, working at the agency for the summer. Today the company would have all left for a fabulous, all-expenses-paid Fourth of July vacation to Turks and Caicos.

It struck her then that not a single one of her employees had boarded that plane today for their well-deserved vacations, despite having fully paid tickets in their hands. Instead, they were all sitting in the waiting room at the hospital, waiting to see if she would live.

A sob worked its way up her throat as Connor's words came back to her. *No one said anything about fair.* Indeed. Nothing about this whole situation seemed fair, least of all that Aubrey should be somehow in danger because of her.

She sniffed. *Pull it together, Emma. No use getting emotional now. That won't help anything.* She was going to figure this out. She had to figure this out. Flicking a look back at Connor, she saw he was watching her again. *Drat.* She definitely didn't need him to see her get emotional. He already thought she was a waste of his time.

He reached down and picked up something in the grass, studying it in his palm.

"What is that?" she called.

He proffered his palm, but she was too far away to see. "This yours?" he asked, arriving beside her in a blink of an eye.

"You have to stop doing that," she said of his warp speed arrival.

"Sorry," he said, holding out the object he'd found in his flattened palm. It was a seventies-style peace-symbol necklace, made of real silver, that bore a gaudy-looking green stone at its center. A bit of memorabilia—not worth a dollar, probably, but invaluable to her niece.

"It's Aubrey's," she told him.

"'Twas near where your car landed."

Emma inspected it. "She never takes it off. I can't imagine what it's doing here. It belonged to her mother, Lizzy. But Aubrey wasn't here that night."

"No, she wasn't. Only you and those three others. Plus the emergency workers who came to help ye."

"*Three* others?"

"Countin' the one who found you. The one who didna call for help?"

"How do you know about him?"

"I was standin' right beside you that night after the crash."

Emma's lips parted in surprise. He'd seemed to appear from nowhere that night, but he'd been listening to everything. To those men talking on the hillside. That, she remembered. "You were?"

"Aye. Though I didn't show myself to ye right away. I was waitin' to…" He hesitated.

"To what?"

"To hear ye speak."

She frowned. "And when I did?"

"Ye sounded like her."

"Like Violet." Not a question. She already knew the answer.

"Aye," he said, pocketing the necklace. "Just like her."

"And I look like her, too?"

He nodded, scanning her features and lifting his fingers to her face, touching a spot near her eye. "Mostly. A modern version. Except here. And here," he said, pushing a strand of hair from her eyes. With that, he walked up the hillside partway, and she followed.

"That's quite a coincidence."

He shrugged but said nothing. Instead, he scanned the ground again nearby.

"Maybe I should be asking a different question," she said, following him. "Maybe I should ask how I became your person? Why are you assigned to me if you have such strong feelings about *her*? Bad feelings, that is."

"'Tis a punishment, I ken," he said but sent her a side-eye.

Emma sniffed and echoed his words under her breath.

What might have passed for amusement twisted his mouth, which also might have been the first time he'd nearly smiled at her.

"So, this Violet person. Was she an angel, too?"

He barked a humorless laugh. "Hardly."

"So, then, before you were an angel, you were…?"

"A Scot," he growled—rather proudly, it seemed to her.

"I was going to say human."

He shrugged, acknowledging it. Reaching down into the long grass, he picked up something else that caught his eye.

She gasped. "My shoe!" She reached for the other half of her way-too-expensive brown-and-blue Gucci sandals, only to have her fingers pass through it. She let out a growl of frustration. "That's just wrong. I can't even put it on now that I've found it!"

"I suppose I'll just have t' keep judgin' ye, then, for yer poor wee bare foot."

Emma clapped a shocked hand to her chest. "Wait. Was that a joke?"

He made a face. "No." But he still grinned as he turned away from her.

"I think we're making progress, don't you?"

For his part, Connor wouldn't give her that. Yet. He looked up as a still-dappled fawn stepped into the meadow just beyond where they stood, her wet black nose in the air. She took a few tentative steps toward Emma.

"Look at that," Emma whispered. "I think she sees us, too."

"She does," he answered. "They don't fear us as they do mortals." He reached his hand out to her, and she walked up to sniff it. As easily as one would pet a dog or a cat, he reached out to scratch her behind the ears. "We mean them no harm."

Emma's gaze went soft, surveying the accident scene. "A shame people can't figure out that simple skill."

"Aye, a true shame," he said with an accusing look at her. Though the moment he uttered those, he regretted them. His kneejerk response to her was feeling considerably less deserved than it had been only hours ago because it was clear she had no memory of him at all.

His words were met with a weary expression. "We should go," she told him, digging her bare toe into the long grass. "I thought I would remember whatever it was I forgot if I came here. But I…can't. I'm sorry I dragged you here."

"I believe 'twas I who dragged you," he said.

Emma's eyes went suddenly wide. Her face paled. "Oh!"

"Emma?"

She touched her hand to her head. "I—I feel—"

He reached for her arm as she swayed, but then she disappeared. Completely.

"*Emma?*" Connor whirled around, looking for her as the fawn scampered back into the woods, but she was gone. A sinking feeling hit him squarely in the gut.

There were only two reasons for her to vanish that way. And he liked neither one.

Chapter Four

MARGUERITE CIEL SAT on the edge of the hospital rooftop ledge, her legs dangling off the side, her face to the sweet, ocean-flavored westerly breeze that came with the setting sun. From here, the Pacific stretched across to the horizon, broken only by the lines of surf that marched across the ocean like soldiers and the seabirds that circled above it. Marguerite's dog, Enoch, sat beside her, watching the birds.

"Ahhh," Marguerite sighed, "there is almost nothing better than this view, right here, on the whole earth. Don't you agree?"

Connor, who was pacing across the loose-rock roof like an agitated fool, said nothing.

"It calms the mind and the heart like nothin' else," she went on. "I do so miss this part of life. I suppose I shall never get over missin' it."

Bracing his palms on the building's ledge, Connor stared down at the people crossing the parking lot below, going back to their lives. Leaving behind whatever had brought them to this place. If only for a while. He'd come up here to clear his head. Marguerite's unexpected visit was a distraction he merely tolerated. His thoughts were on Emma and the crisis that had just gone on in her room downstairs only minutes ago.

A flurry of doctors and nurses had swarmed around her, shoving Aubrey out of the way to do what needed doing. Exactly what they'd done was not in his purview, but they had worked on her for a good ten minutes before stabilizing her again. But Emma—the spirit of Emma—had not returned to him. He couldn't say why, as he sensed her life was still precariously on the edge. Maybe because Marguerite had chosen now to drop in for a chat. What if that short time with Emma was all he'd have? She would either live or die and he would go on to a new assignment, and that would be that.

His chest tightened.

He would miss her contrariness. Her teasing voice. Blast him. Even the way she looked at him.

What business did he have allowing his feelings to get involved?

"That is not like you, Connor," Marguerite said.

"Get out of my head, woman."

She smiled softly at him. "You're surprised. But me, no. Not really."

"Will ye never stop stirrin' the pot?"

"The pot stirring is for your own good, *mon ami*. Too much left undone between you two. It must be tied off once and for all. Or it will always bleed."

"I've no wish to tie anything with her," he lied.

"You mean," she clarified, "with Violet."

He shook his head. "Emma's just…"

"Just what?"

Connor sat on the ledge opposite his mentor, staring out at the orange sun balancing on the horizon. "She's nothing like her. Yet it's as if she's stepped right out of my history."

"You know as well as I that the bargain she struck comin' into this life put you together here. Put her on that dark road that night. Along with all the people she's with here. Partly for this very purpose. To tie off that wound once and for all. If you don't, you'll be seeing her again someday."

"Perhaps," he admitted. "Perhaps I'll never see her again. If she lives." He glanced at the +9 percent on the dial on his wrist.

Marguerite stood to face him. "The Council voted in your favor at the last session. I thought you might want to know."

That got his attention. "In my favor? How is that?"

"One of the members—Esme—has chosen to leave."

"Leave? You mean quit? No one quits." Such a thing was unheard of. The best he could have hoped for was an expansion of the seats. The Council, of which Roland was head, was as high a rank as a guardian could go. There were higher celestials, of course, but his sights had never been set there.

"No," she explained. "She's decided there is important

work for her here."

Connor couldn't quite wrap his mind around this. Of all the Council's thirty-two members, Esme would have been the last one he could imagine giving up the prestige of the Council. "She's falling?" Again, at that level, unheard of.

"No, she will begin anew. She had an *envie* for new adventure."

Adventure. *Och.* That he could understand. Of late, he'd often found himself longing for some adventure after centuries of dailiness as a guardian. The sameness was wearing. Notwithstanding Emma.

The Council seat had been his answer to all that sameness, but now that the possibility had presented itself, now that he'd had his hands in the grass here, Emma's hand in his, had found himself feeling things he hadn't allowed himself to feel for so long, now he wondered. Was the Council seat enough? Was he even enough for them?

Enoch trotted across the ledge to sit down beside him, putting his small, furry head beneath Connor's hand, asking for a pat. He obliged.

"I assume you want the seat?" Marguerite said, breaking into his thoughts. "What shall I tell them?"

Finding the random pebbles on the ledge suddenly of particular interest, he said, "Of course I want it. Ye didna think I'd say otherwise, did ye? It's what I've wanted for a long time."

Even from this vantage, he could feel her slow, sly smile

beside him.

She made a noise, a self-satisfied sound that hardly needed interpretation. "All the same, maybe I'll hold off a bit before giving them your answer. No need to be hasty or to make them think you want it that badly."

He scowled at her. Of course they knew he wanted the seat. Everyone knew he wanted it. "I willna change my mind."

"Then there's no rush, *sha*. You do what you gotta do here. When you get done, you come see me, no?"

"Ye can count on it."

"*Ca c'est bon,*" she said, tucking the little dog under her arm. "Come, Enoch. We've places to be." In the next instant, she and Enoch were gone.

Connor turned back to the sunset, dipping below the horizon. He'd always imagined how he'd feel once he got the call to the Council. Validated? Complete? Maybe even victorious. But what he felt was none of those things. Instead, he doubted—himself, his mission, and even his path. For perhaps the first time, he questioned what he'd thought he wanted all these years. The thought tumbled through him that what he needed might be something completely different.

AUBREY SAT BESIDE her aunt in the ICU, holding her hand.

It seemed impossible that this still, suddenly fragile woman beside her was the same vibrant, ambitious, loving one who'd seen her through the worst time in her life. The last twenty-four hours felt like a nightmare that she couldn't wake up from. The thought of living without Emma was unbearable. Aside from loving her like crazy and planning for their futures together like sisters, she was Aubrey's last and only connection to her parents.

She tried not to dwell on her parents' deaths—or most especially the way they'd died. But sitting in the ICU with Emma brought that trauma rushing back. Not even Jacob's calm presence could soothe her.

She squeezed Emma's hand. "They're going to make me leave soon," she told her. "I want you to know I'm here, though. I wish you could hear me, Emma. I don't say this enough. I love you. I've always loved you. You're my favorite—my only—aunt." That would have made Emma laugh if she'd heard it, but it only made tears form in Aubrey's eyes. "I'm so tired, Em. I'm so very tired of losing people. I'm glad you're fighting. But please, don't scare me like that again."

The glass door to the room slid open, and someone entered behind her. She didn't bother to look because she knew it was a nurse, come to ask her to go. But as he came around the side of Emma's bed, she saw it was a male nurse in blue scrubs whom she'd never seen before. His name tag read *Joseph Lassiter, RN.* Something about him startled her. Maybe it was his too-long hair or the fact that he might've been one of the most handsome men with whom she'd crossed paths in a long time. With the exception of Jacob.

Joseph smiled at her as he reached up to check Emma's IV drip, inspecting it but not adjusting it. "Yer her niece, then? Yer all right?"

Of course he had a Scottish accent. Of course he did. "Yes. No. Well, it's hard to say," she admitted with a shake of her head.

"I ken 'tis hard."

"I haven't seen you before," she said, making conversation to direct it away from herself.

"Just got on shift," he said without meeting her eye. He glanced down at his name tag. "I'm…uh, Joseph. Joseph Lassiter."

She nodded. "Aubrey. Have you talked to her doctors, then, Joseph? Do you know anything more? What are they saying?"

"She's a fighter, that one. Or so I hear. It's a waitin' game, is all." He turned his beautiful face fully toward her now. "But ye look tired. How long have ye been here now?"

"Since last night. I should go home, shower, change my—"

"*Och, no,*" he said abruptly. "I mean, I'm verra sure we could find a spot for you to rest here. If ye want to, that is."

"Really? I don't know. I can't really think straight." She rubbed her aching forehead. It was surprising. So kind of him to offer. But she really wanted to change her clothes and eat something besides vending-machine coffee and candy bars.

"Might be best." He shot a concerned look at her, as if convincing her of that was as important as his job taking care of Emma—his patient.

Fear punched through her brain fog. "Are you saying that because you think something bad might happen again tonight? You think I shouldn't go?"

"No, no. I'm only sayin' it might be easiest for you to stay close if I can find ye a bed. Send your fella, Jacob, out to your place. Pick up your things?"

"You…you've met Jacob?"

"He's worried for ye," he said, studying Emma's face as he absently lifted the clipboard from where it hung. "Good lad. He asked me to talk ye into a rest."

It was true that Jacob had been trying for the last few hours to get her to lie down somewhere.

Joseph lifted Emma's wrist to take her pulse, despite the beeping monitor a few steps away. It might have just been her imagination that he rubbed his thumb gently against the back of Emma's hand before releasing it.

Their eyes met for an instant. His were a gray-blue color she'd honestly never seen before. There was something…luminous about him. Something different.

"I'll go look for a room for ye, all right? Ye can have a shower? A wee nap."

"Thank you, Joseph. I really appreciate that. You're from

Scotland, aren't you?" She wasn't sure why she'd asked him. Just to make conversation, she supposed. Or to prolong the inevitable.

He shrugged. "But not for a long time. What gave me away?" he asked with a grin.

"Oh, I don't know. I think all you need is a kilt to go with that accent. It's charming."

"Or perhaps I can find me a wee bagpiper to follow me around so there'll be no confusion."

She laughed. It felt good to laugh after the day she'd had. "I'd like to see that."

"So would I," he said. "I'll look after her now. Try not to worry."

"Please try to help her live."

With the briefest flicker of a smile in Emma's direction, he nodded, then left the room.

It was probably just that she was so tired that she couldn't put her finger on what exactly felt odd about that encounter. Except that most of the nurses kept their thoughts to themselves, unlike Joseph Lassiter, who'd gone out of his way to be kind. But she made a mental note to remember his name. She wanted to make sure she thanked him later.

CONNOR TORE OFF Joseph Lassiter's name tag from the

scrubs he'd requisitioned from the nurse's lounge as he made his way down the corridor. On the way, he buttonholed an orderly who agreed to arrange for a place for Aubrey to rest. It took no time at all to convince the thin, young orderly that it was his own idea, after all. Humans were so easy.

That done, he pressed the elevator button and entered alone, reverting back to his guardian form before the car hit the next floor.

Twice in one day was some kind of record for him. First for Winston, then for Aubrey. Or rather, for Emma. He shook his head. Yes, he'd done it for her, knowing how concerned she was for Aubrey's safety. Allowing Emma's niece to walk solo into the mess at Emma's home was not an option. If whoever had torn apart Emma's home hadn't found what they were looking for, Aubrey wasn't safe going back. It seemed the least he could do to enlist Jacob to walk into the chaos first.

But doing Emma the small kindness of protecting Aubrey didn't mean he'd changed his mind about her aunt. No. It only meant that he was doing his job. No matter what Marguerite thought.

And even though Emma appeared to have transformed in the intervening centuries, he couldn't bring himself to forgive her. Or trust her.

A soul was a soul was a soul.

As the elevator descended, he remembered the first time he'd met Violet.

She'd been the oldest girl of eight, after all three of her brothers had died in infancy. By default, perhaps, or more likely by force of personality, she became her father's chosen one, his hope for the future, what remained of his line following his wife's death. A scholar and barrister, Callum Gray had taught his brilliant daughter to read and write, an unusual skill most men had found useless, if not threatening. Connor had known her from the time he was ten when she'd arrived at his father's estate alongside Callum Gray, riding her unruly pony, Duchess. The horse's name had amused him endlessly. But after Violet had climbed to the top of the willow tree beside the pond to prove a point to his younger brother, Arthur, Connor had needed little to convince him that they would become friends. Later, much more than friends.

If he closed his eyes, a thousand memories would reappear of her, the adventures they'd had as children, especially climbing amongst the ruins of the ancient Narwick Castle that sat abandoned in the hills above the Montrose estate. It was there the two of them would endlessly plot their futures where the wide Scottish sky met the moors of heather. The second son of a duke, Connor's path was already set. It would take him into the military where he would prove himself, then build his own wealth as a soldier. Violet had longed for nothing more than to follow in her father's footsteps, attend university, to write treatises and histories of the country she loved.

All that would change when Connor's older brother, Edgar, died. Connor had become heir apparent.

The military would not be his path, but he would be the next duke of Montrose. Somewhere between the ruins and the sea cliffs, he and Violet would see their future together.

They'd shared their first kiss there in the heather fields. It was there he'd asked her to be his wife. Her eyes had been the color of the moors in autumn, a dark-haired beauty whom men had coveted and pursued. But it was he who had won her heart. She was to be *his* wife. At least, he'd thought so.

The doors to the elevator swished open. Emma was standing on the other side.

"Connor!" She flung herself at him in a hug as effervescent as it was unexpected. "Oh, I couldn't find you anywhere!"

Relief poured through him, too. Though he could hardly admit to himself that the thought of never seeing her again like this had struck a coldness through him. A dread.

To feel her in his arms again, her breasts pushed up against the wall of his chest, her breath, warm against his neck, tightened his gut. It also sent an unwelcome heat to his groin. *Och*, he'd been haunted trying to remember the feel of her in his arms for centuries, and now…

It took him a moment to remember himself.

"I was so scared when I woke and you were gone," she whispered against his chest. "I don't know what happened."

Her mortal counterparts swirled around them, going about their business as the two of them stood in the middle of the hallway embracing, two rocks in a swirling stream.

Gently, he set her away from him, his gaze on her damp cheeks and the fear in her eyes. "Dinna worry. I am here for it all."

"Did I…did I die?"

"There was some trouble. Do ye not recall it?"

She shook her head. "Only that one minute I was talking to you in the field and the next I woke in the hospital looking for you. But you were gone. Aubrey was gone, and Jacob—"

"That'd be my doin'."

She looked at him strangely.

"I might've spoken to yer niece and to Jacob."

Her eyes widened. She grabbed his hand to drag him toward the window in the hallway where they could have some privacy. Not that anyone could hear them.

"You *spoke* to them?"

"Aye. As I said, 'tis possible, now and then, to appear as one of ye. No one kens the difference."

"Wait, so Aubrey talked to you?"

"She did."

"What did she say?" she asked this urgently, desperate to hear the answer.

"She's worried about ye. Ye already know she loves ye madly."

Emma nodded. "And I, her. I'm not sure how she'd do without me."

"'Tis not for you to fix, Emma. Aubrey has her own angels lookin' out for her."

"Does she?" She shot a hopeful look at him. "Of course she does. But it's good to hear you say that." She sat on the ledge of the window with the halo of the outdoor streetlamps behind her. "It's funny how a day can change everything. One quick accident and all I thought was true, all I believed is different now. Here I am, with you, and everything is upside down."

"Not everything," he said with a half smile. "You're upright again. I sent Aubrey to a room to get some rest. Jacob went to your home to get her some things."

"But when he gets there, he'll see…"

Connor nodded. "Better him than Aubrey. Best not to have her run smack into that alone. Not until we uncover who was behind it."

She looked surprised. "We?"

He shrugged, staring out into the dark night. "I canna see ye doin' it alone."

Impulsively, she curled her fingers around his arm. "You'll help me, then?"

Her touch sent an inexplicable, unwelcome shudder of want through him. "I will," he said. "For as long as I can."

She swallowed thickly. "Thank you, Connor."

The look of gratitude in her eyes was almost more than

he could bear. "'Tis my job."

She knew as well as he how those words were meant to land. "Of course." She dropped her hand and turned toward the window. "Why else would you help me?"

Now he'd stepped in it. He couldn't seem to help himself when it came to her.

"'Tis wrong o' me to hold Violet against you, I know," he said, standing close to her, searching the darkness for what she was seeing.

"Just so you know, I have no idea who this Violet person is or how she hurt you, but I assure you I had nothing to do with her."

Connor scratched his head, then shoved his hair out of his eyes. "That's not exactly true. Because, Emma…you are, in fact, Violet."

Chapter Five

EMMA TURNED TO Connor, dumbstruck. "What in the world are you talking about?"

"You are Violet and Violet is you."

She snorted. "Maybe I'm not the only one with a head injury here."

"You've no memory of that life. But your soul is hers. Here on Earth, once again, looking...nearly the same."

A frown tugged at her brow. "Are you saying...I've lived before?"

"What it is goes by many names," he allowed. "But 'tis a choice the soul makes."

"And I chose to return." She gestured to her body. "As this?"

"And I"—he spread his arms wide—"am this."

She was about to question him further, when Jacob came running down the hallway, a look of panic on his face.

She and Connor exchanged looks, knowing he'd seen the house. Emma followed him. Connor did, too.

At the ICU, Jacob skidded to a stop at Emma's glass door. Sweat stained the front of his shirt as if he'd been running. "Where is Aubrey?" Jacob asked no one in particular. "Where's my girlfriend?" He turned to the nurse sitting at the nurses' station. "Have you seen Aubrey? I need to find her."

"It's okay," the nurse they knew as Riley told him, coming around the desk to calm him down. "Aubrey is resting. She's fine."

Nearly breathless, he braced his hands on the desk. "Are you sure? Where is she?"

"We found a bed for her on the next floor down, in the—"

Before she could even finish the sentence, Jacob was running toward the open elevator doors.

Riley called after him. "I can call down to the nurses' station for you—"

But he was already pushing buttons. Riley picked up the phone anyway and called down.

By the time they'd found Jacob downstairs, he was banging an impatient hand on the nursing supervisor's desk as she pointed down the hall to a closed door.

He burst through the door of the room where Aubrey was sleeping. She shot up in bed, eyes wide with surprise. "Jacob! Wha—?"

Jacob sagged with relief at the door before sitting down beside her on the bed. "Thank God."

"What's wrong? Are you all right? You're...you're scaring me."

"I couldn't find you," he said, gathering his breath. "I needed to find you." He took her hand.

"You knew they were letting me rest here."

"Yeah, I knew. But…listen to me. Something happened."

"What?"

"Emma's house. Your house—"

"What about it?" She squeezed his hand now, looking scared, too.

"Someone…someone tore it apart. It's a mess. There's stuff everywhere."

"Wait, what?"

"I don't think it's a simple robbery. That would be a big freakin' coincidence. They didn't even take the usual stuff. TVs. Computers—"

"Oh my God."

"—jewelry, even. It was all there. I don't know what they took or what they were looking for. Your room was tossed, too. I mean, it's bad. Winston's still there," he said, rubbing his forehead. "Looks like these freaks actually fed him, too."

"*What?*"

"Yeah, there was a pile of dry food on the floor. A fresh bowl of water. No way he got that food out of that closed Tupperware thing by himself."

Emma slid a look at Connor, who shrugged.

"Winston," Aubrey breathed. "I forgot all about him in this craziness. Was he okay?"

"Freaked out, but yeah. Okay. But the house, Aubrey. It just proves that what happened to Emma was no accident. Someone is after her. After something she has."

"Did you call the police?"

He shook his head. "I had this feeling, this panic that whoever is after her might hurt you."

"Why would they? I have nothing."

"Anyway, I'm calling the police," he said, pulling his phone from his pocket. "And I'm going to get them to send someone over here."

"Do you think Emma's still in danger?"

Jacob swallowed hard. "Now I do."

He'd worked for the local prosecutor's office prosecuting criminal cases in their smallish town for the last three years. If Jacob was worried, they should all be worried.

"None of this makes any sense," Aubrey told him as they left the small room together. "I mean, I could have as easily been driving there that night."

"What?"

"Do you remember that I was supposed to be taking that meeting Emma was on her way to? With the seller of that penthouse down by the beach? You asked me to come to dinner to meet your parents instead?"

"Right. You felt bad about ducking out on Emma. But she was okay with it."

"That meeting had been set up for days, and Emma had wanted me to do it because she thought it would be good experience for me to close that deal. Bruce Waller, the owner, was close to signing a sales contract, and since I'd been doing a lot of the negotiating, Emma wanted me to close. But, of course, she let me go with you instead. But it would have been me going that night. I would have been driving Emma's car, with mine still in the shop. We've been sharing her car for weeks. It could have been me."

Emma shook her head, moving closer to Aubrey. "No, Aubrey…that's—"

The possibility seemed to shake him. "But why would anyone want to hurt either one of you? That's the question that needs an answer. What were they doing in your house, and what were they looking for?"

"That *is* the question," Connor said, leaning closer to Emma as they followed the pair down the hallway. "Can ye not think of anything?"

She shook her head. "They didn't even take anything I could see. What could they want?"

"Somethin' ye don't see as valuable?" he suggested, ushering her onto the elevator alongside Aubrey and Jacob, who had no idea they had company.

"But if they were after some*thing*," Emma said. "Why try to kill me to get it? Why not just break into my house when we're gone?"

"What if they thought ye had it wi' you?"

"But I didn't. I had nothing of any value with me. Nothing."

He tipped a look at her niece. "What if they thought Aubrey did? What if they thought it was her in the car?"

"But…she's practically a college student. Her parents left her with virtually nothing. I'm all she has. What could they possibly want?"

They turned to look at the young woman who was cradled against her boyfriend's shoulder.

Connor said, "Perhaps we need to figure out the 'they' before we can figure out the 'what.'"

THE POLICE INTERVIEWED both Aubrey and Jacob again. Another team investigated the break-in at Emma's home. But they seemed no closer in figuring out what had happened or why. The "who" was just as mysterious as the rest. The police had taken impressions of tire marks at the scene and had a make and model of car that had run Emma off the road, based on the paint scraped off her car. But there were a thousand cars like that in this part of the state. Narrowing that down seemed a herculean task.

Emma had watched all of this with a sick feeling in the pit of her stomach. It seemed like some clock was ticking down. She just might run out of time to protect Aubrey.

Connor either didn't know or wouldn't say whether Emma herself would live or die, but she had resigned herself to being in the moment now. There was no use worrying about death while she still had time to live.

"Connor?" she said as they watched the sun rise the next morning. Orange feathered the dark blue sky in wispy streaks that brightened as they watched.

"Aye?"

"If I live, after all of this will I remember you?" Her voice broke the tiniest bit as she asked the question. The notion that she would forget him seemed impossible.

"Hard t' say." He peered out the window harder, as if something had caught his attention.

"What does that mean exactly?"

"To be truthful, mortals who encounter us down here…when we're physical…canna remember after. Their memory of such a thing disappears. 'Tis a protection for ye, after all."

"It must be a rare thing, I suppose."

"Now and then," he said with a shrug, "we're allowed a mingle. We stay for a time as nearly mortals. 'Tis usually for a task that needs doin', canna be done any other way."

"You've done one of these *mingles*?"

"I've done them." A muscle worked in his jaw.

"So, will I remember you?"

He turned her way at last, his beautiful eyes fixing on hers. "I will remember you."

Her heart gave a heavy thump, and for a moment, she thought he meant to kiss her. His gaze scanned her face, her mouth, the way she moistened her lips with her tongue. She closed her eyes, leaning closer, parting her lips for that kiss. But a humiliating heartbeat later, she opened her eyes to find he'd turned away again.

"Wow. Even in the in-between," she murmured, "I can't seem to get my timing right."

He seemed embarrassed somehow, not at all like the arrogant angel who'd spent the last day or so feeling righteous. "'Tis naught to do with ye, Emma. I canna."

"You *'canna'* what? Kiss me? Have feelings for me?"

"'Course I have feelin's for ye."

"Bad feelings, maybe. Or indifferent. That's fine. I mean, I'm practically dead. What can I expect?"

"I'm a celestial and you're a mortal—more or less—and those two things, they canna be…together."

"But I'm not exactly mortal here, am I, Farm Boy? I can't hold a spoon between my fingers, but I can hold your hand. So, what does that make me? A temporary distraction?"

He slid a dark look at her, clearly wanting to say something but holding back.

"I'm sorry," she said, shaking her head. "Don't mind me. I'm just going through something here. Anyway, kissing is such a mortal thing. Unnecessary, really. And pointless."

Without a beat of warning, he pulled her to him and proceeded to refute that point. Wrapping his powerful arms around her, his mouth moved over hers with the hunger of a man who'd starved himself for too long and had found his salvation, kissing her deeply and without any of the caution he'd only a moment ago been preaching.

Stunned, Emma swayed in his embrace, her knees going weak as he leaned her backward in the cradle of his arms. There was anger in his kiss, but she didn't care about that, either. She felt her stomach drop and flutter as heat impaled her from the core of her being, outward toward every part of her. As he plundered her mouth, she did the same to his, clinging to him, her fingers tucked into the long curls at the base of his neck, her lungs breathing in the sweet scent of him. All the while, there was a buzzing, something electrical and glittery moving through them. Some stirring of an old sparkle of memory that echoed inside her for only a moment before he lifted his mouth from hers.

Still holding her, his face only a breath from hers, he spoke to her without saying a word aloud. *"Dinna think I haven't imagined this every day for centuries. Dinna think I haven't wanted to taste ye again. And now I have."*

His voice. It reached right inside her. She wasn't sure her legs would hold her as he set her away from him. She crumpled onto the window ledge, leaning back against the glass, still catching her breath. "That was quite a kiss…for being impossible." She grinned up at him through her lashes. "Apparently you haven't lost your touch."

"My self-control is another matter altogether."

Another shiver of heat chased across her skin as his gaze raked over her. "I'm of the opinion that self-control is often overrated."

"Not in my case."

"Regardless," she told him, "I won't forget it. No matter what happens."

A half smile curved his mouth, but his gaze caught sight of something outside. She followed his look. A man, a familiar-looking man with blond hair and a slim build, was walking across the parking lot, holding a bouquet of flowers.

She jumped to her feet. *Holy old boyfriends!* Could she have conjured him up with her thoughts about him the other day back at the car? The boy who'd started the whole kissing ballgame rolling all those years ago?

Connor raised a disapproving brow. "Who's that?"

"Someone I used to know." *Surely he's not here to visit me. Oh, please, don't let him be coming to see me.* Automatically, she reached a hand up to straighten out her hair, only belatedly realizing it would do nothing to improve the appearance of the other Emma, lying in the bed.

Connor took her hand. A moment later, they were standing at her bedside near Aubrey and Jacob. They both looked exhausted.

A nurse popped her head in the door. "There's someone to see you, Aubrey. He's just outside in the waiting area. Says his name is Aaron."

With an uncertain frown, Aubrey followed her to where Aaron was waiting.

He smiled, holding the flowers out toward her as she approached. Emma thought fourteen years had been good to him. He had grown into his body, his face angled instead of rounded. His smile, kind as ever. How had they let so much time pass between them?

"Aubrey, I don't know if you remember me," he said, holding out the flowers to her. "Aaron Pleasure. I'm an old friend of Emma's. You and I—we spoke after your parents…"

"Yes. Aaron. How lovely of you to think of her."

He handed her the flowers wrapped in florist paper.

"Thank you for these. I'll make sure to find a vase for them. By the way, it was so kind of you to send flowers for my parents' service."

"Of course," he said. "How's Em?"

"The same. She's in a coma. We don't really know what's going to happen."

"Right." He gestured to a chair there in the waiting area, where they sat down. "I'm very sorry you're going through this again. And for Em. She doesn't deserve this. I just happened to be in town to see family. I'm in Palo Alto now—California—and I heard about her accident from a friend. Terrible. It shook me. I wanted to come by and—"

"It wasn't an accident. At least, we're pretty sure it wasn't," Aubrey told him.

He blinked. "What?"

"We think she was driven off the road intentionally. They found pieces of the other car apparently. A dark gray

SUV, they think. But you know, there are a million of those. Finding the 'one' may be like…like finding a needle in the haystack."

"But they think it was intentional? Why would someone do that?"

"I don't know. No one knows."

"Jeez, Aubrey. I'm…sorry."

"Thanks," she said. "Hopefully, the police will figure it out."

"If there's anything I can do—"

"Say a prayer? It was nice of you to stop by. I'd let you see her, but she'd probably kill me if I did. Nothing personal. She's a little vain."

Emma's eyes widened with affront. "*Vain?* I am not!"

"Well," Connor pointed out. "You did say yourself ye didn't want him to see ye like this."

"No, I didn't." Emma narrowed a look at him. "Well, I may have thought that, but I never said it aloud." Her expression flattened. "Are you reading my mind again?"

He lifted his hands a smidge.

With a huff of exasperation, she turned her attention back to Aaron, who was talking about Lizzy now.

"…I stayed in touch for a long time with Lizzy and Dan. She knew I was always interested to hear about the shipwrecks they were exploring and what they'd found. Your parents were my aspirational adventure heroes while I sat writing code at my desk in Silicon Valley. I can't tell you how crushing it was to hear about their deaths."

"Crushing. Yes," Aubrey said, her eyes shiny with moisture. "It was. They loved their treasure hunts. They died doing it."

Connor turned a curious look on Emma. She answered with a quelling head shake.

Thankfully, Aaron didn't ask for details about Lizzy and Daniel's deaths. Not that Aubrey would know the answers, but he had grace enough not to press her right now on another painful topic. She was already going through enough.

Aaron stared down at his feet. "So often, over the years, I've wanted to get in touch with Emma. One thing after the other, I guess. I'd like to think she knew I was thinking of her, though."

"She talked about you often," Aubrey said. "When we'd hike up on the cliffs, she'd tell me all the stories about you two. She's always thought of you very fondly."

"I still do. I'm not dead yet," Emma murmured, standing close to Aaron now. She flicked a look up at Connor, whose expression had gone curiously dark.

"Thank you for the flowers," Aubrey told Aaron. "I know she will appreciate them when she wakes up."

"I do," Emma murmured.

"I'm in town for a week or so. I'll stop by again. I hope…I'm sure she'll be awake then." He handed her a business card. "If you need anything, Aubrey…"

"Thanks, Aaron. For stopping by."

He kissed her cheek, then walked down the hallway.

Emma watched him until he'd disappeared around the corner. "Why do we procrastinate doing things that are important? I should have gotten in touch with him myself, but I didn't, either."

"Do ye find it a wee bit odd that he should show up here just now?"

"What do you mean?" she asked as Aubrey headed back to Emma's room.

Connor stared down the hall after Aaron. "I mean I dinna believe in coincidence."

It took her a few beats to catch up with him. "What are you implying? That he could have had something to do with my accident?"

He shrugged noncommittally. "Might've."

"Aaron? You can't possibly think—?"

"It's been years since he last saw ye. Last…kissed ye."

She felt her cheeks heat. How could he know that? And what difference could it possibly… "Are you—? You can't be jealous?"

"*Jealous? Och*, no. I'm only sayin'—"

"That because he came to see *me*, he must have some ulterior motive?"

"Well, someone has it in for you or Aubrey. Knows somethin' about ye."

"There's an old saying that if you hear hoofbeats, you

should be looking for horses, not zebras."

His jaw worked. "I dinna ken what that means, but—"

"Aaron is a zebra," she informed him. "He would *never*."

"And," he added, "your zebra, Aaron, also knew your sister, Lizzy."

"So what if he did?"

"Maybe ye should tell me how she died, your sister."

Emma braced her hands on her hips. "Don't you know? You know everything."

"No," he said. "I don't. 'Tis not my job to keep track of all the souls. That would'a been Elspeth's job." Almost instantly, she could see he regretted bringing up her name.

"Who's Elspeth?"

"A friend of mine. Ex-keeper of the Celestial files. She had a knack for it. She rarely forgot anything. Some kind of a photographic mind, she had."

"Had? Where is she now?"

Now he really looked uncomfortable. "Retired."

"Is she a guardian like you, then?"

"Not anymore."

"What happened to her?" Emma asked.

"Nothin' happened to her. 'Twas her choice. She's mortal. For good."

Emma shook her head, confused. "She's—? How...how is that?"

"'Tis no' important." Connor started toward the ICU, but she followed close on his heels, dodging wheelchairs and nurses walking down the hall. "That's only on a need-to-know basis."

"Well, I need to know. How exactly is she down here for good?"

There was the scent of antiseptic in the air, of sterilized sheets and the sound of TVs coming from rooms they passed. Nurses chatted in the nurses' station, answering questions of patients' families that waited nearby. But all of that was just a distracting hum in the background. Emma could hardly keep up with Connor's steps, but she wasn't about to let this go.

"Tell me."

"Why?" he demanded.

"Why did you bring her up?"

"Because you—" He turned abruptly on her. "She fell, all right? Because she decided to. Remember the mingle I told you about?"

She nodded.

"That's what happened. She wanted to stay. She met a man. A mortal. It was meant to be."

"And she fell?"

"Aye."

"And you miss her." It was not a question. There was a sadness in his eyes as he told her. Maybe a bittersweet sadness.

He shrugged. "Aye. But…'tis all right."

They reached Emma's floor and moved down the hallway. "Have you seen Elspeth since she…fell?"

With the shake of his head, he closed the subject. But she couldn't stop thinking about his friend falling. An angel falling. Becoming human. Was it common? Rare? Were there people she knew who had fallen? Could one intersect with an angel—a guardian—and not even know it? Of course, Aubrey had just today with Connor in the guise of a male nurse.

"What did Aaron want?" Jacob asked Aubrey outside Emma's room when she returned.

"Flowers for Emma. He was a friend of hers. A long time ago."

"And Kinsey brought these by," he said, holding up another bouquet. A cheery mix of peonies, tulips, and pink roses mixed with baby's breath. The fragrance of the flowers cut the sting of the sterile hospital smell. This was the second expensive bouquet she'd brought since Emma had been hospitalized. But the ICU frowned on flowers in the room. They'd have to take them back home.

"That's very nice of her," Aubrey said. "And not to point fingers, but it's a little unusual for Kinsey, who rarely seems to notice anyone outside her own little box."

"That's kind of true," Emma allowed.

"I don't know," Jacob mused. "She seems genuinely broken up about Emma's accident. You just never know what's going on inside someone like Kinsey."

"That's the understatement of the year. Kinsey's loyal to

Emma, but flowers? That so isn't like her."

"Sue Marti stopped by earlier, too, to see if you needed anything. She's bringing you some soup tomorrow, staffing the Brandon's Hope Home Tour this weekend. She's apparently got it all under control. She said, and I quote, 'It's already a screaming success.'"

Emma smiled to herself. Brandon's Hope was a fundraising nonprofit that benefited children's cancer research. Every year, Emma arranged for one or two of the beautiful homes she'd brokered to be perfectly staged for house tours. People paid big bucks to see homes like these, and Emma loved doing it. Their tours had raised almost three hundred thousand dollars since they'd started five years ago.

"Now *that* doesn't surprise me. Good for her."

Worry creased Jacob's expression. "But listen, Aub. I'm worried about Emma's safety. And yours. I don't think she should have any visitors until we figure this thing out."

"I think you're overreacting about this," she told him.

"I'm not. I'm worried about you."

Aubrey rubbed her forehead. "I won't let whoever did this make me a victim."

"You already are," Jacob told her. "I don't want anything to happen to you."

Taking his hand, she said, "I'm a big girl. I can take care of myself."

Emma moved close to Aubrey. "No, you can't. Listen to him."

Jacob frowned. "Whoever did this, Aub? They're not messing around. They nearly killed Emma. They could do the same to you. What if you're right about them mistaking Emma for you?"

"I still can't wrap my brain around why."

"Nor can I," Emma murmured. She glanced at Connor, who was staring down at the Emma in the bed. She couldn't read his expression except it read as conflicted, as it usually did when he looked at her. Who was he seeing? Her or Violet?

"The police want to know if they took anything," Jacob continued. "We're going to have to go back. You're going to have to go back. With me."

"Now?" Aubrey said. "But I need to be here."

Emma leaned close to her ear. "Aubrey," she said, using one of their favorite Oda Mae Brown lines from *Ghost*, "you in danger, girl." That line used to make Aubrey laugh, even when Emma had been grounding her for some infraction or other as a teenager. If only she could laugh her way out of this mess.

But in the end, he convinced her, and Aubrey agreed to go. Emma watched with Connor as they left the hospital to go back to her house.

Emma stared down at her body on the bed. She felt very separate from that Emma. Disconnected almost. That Emma looked frail, vulnerable. Not at all like who she thought herself to be. Most of her life, she'd been called willful, headstrong—words, she suddenly realized, that were rarely, if ever, used to describe a man. She was all of those things, but in a good way. But now no one would look at her and think of that other Emma she had been only two days ago.

"Look at me. I look awful. Am I dying?" she asked Connor again.

"Do ye feel like you are?" he asked, his gray eyes going dark as they swept over her form lying in the bed.

"I don't know. How does it feel to die?"

Her question caught him off guard. For the briefest moments, a flicker of pain crossed his expression. "Come with me," he said, taking her hand in his.

"Where are we going?"

"You'll see."

Chapter Six

BEFORE SHE COULD blink, she found herself in a place that seemed as far away from that stifling room at the hospital as she could be. They stood together at the top of a knell above a vast field that reached toward the sea in the distance.

Toto, we are not in Kansas anymore.

The rolling land below them, scored in a thousand hues of green, pink, lavender, and purple, was covered in flowers of some sort. The fragrance of all of that was wrapped up in a ball of woodsy, sweet, and salty air.

Emma inhaled deeply of the intoxicating scent.

"Where are we?" she asked, scanning the unfamiliar landscape in surprise. "Is this…heaven?"

He laughed, the sound shockingly unfamiliar to her, but it brought a smile to her lips.

"No," he said, gazing out at the spectacle before them. "'Tis Scotland."

Emma's eyes widened. "Scotland? But how…?"

"Ye must disremember all the limits ye know for now," he said. "There's nothing bindin' ye to the way things were."

He was right about that. There was nothing familiar in the way things worked in this in-between world. Connor's steady presence was her only anchor to the life she'd known. Yet she could still feel the brush of heather against her legs. Take in the heady fragrance of the sea and the mossy sweetness of the summer bloom. Feel his skin against her own when he held her hand. Somehow, she'd imagined—when she'd even allowed herself to imagine such things—that all those things would disappear in spirit, that it would all be more ephemeral. That she would never look at a man the way she did Connor and long for him to touch her again.

She stared out at the endless blue sea beyond the cliffs and the road that cut across the moor. A solitary car—the only sign that they had not left the real world behind them—was making its way toward an impressive looking, centuries-old estate atop the enormous cliffs that spilled into the sea, two miles away.

Connor stood beside her, knee deep in those purple flowers, staring, too. He looked like he belonged here, in this very picture of what she'd always imagined Scotland to be.

"It's beautiful," she said, her voice tinged with awe.

"Aye, it is."

"This place, it was your home." It wasn't a question. She already knew the answer somehow.

He pointed to that great estate in the distance. "It stands yet. I grew up here roaming these very moors." He slid a look at her. "Can ye recall it?"

She shook her head. "No. I've never been to Scotland before."

He tugged her toward the hill behind them and an ancient ruin, blackened by time and weather, half-covered in mossy green vines that still stood watch over the valley.

"Wow," she breathed, finding words inadequate at the sight of it.

"'Tis Narwick Castle. Or it was once. Here since the Vikings ruled this land."

They hiked for a few minutes before reaching the fallen stones, half-standing walls and stairways leading to the sky. Together they climbed stones that ended on a wind-scoured battlement wall of gray stone. It felt magical to be standing where warriors must have stood hundreds and hundreds of years ago. On this very spot. Whole lives played out here for a season, then faded away like the heather blooms must every year with the snow.

A prickle of déjà vu niggled at her as she turned to look at Connor, sitting atop a stone wall, staring at her. His handsome face etched with Scottish sunlight, his dark hair whipping across his forehead with the sexiest carelessness. Had she stood in this very spot before? Like this? With him?

Impossible.

But was it?

"No," he said, answering her unasked question. "I kissed ye here. For the first time. When ye were Violet."

She blinked at him, unable to put together words.

"It was here I loved ye. Gave myself to ye. And you to me. Here on these very stones." He scratched off a vine from the stone revealing initials carved there.

VG + CM

"Violet Gray and Connor Montrose," he said.

Emma's lips parted as the sensation of déjà vu grew stronger. She could almost see the look in Connor's eyes, rising above her, his hair falling across his cheek as he drove into her. The twist and plunge of desire awakened in her belly. The remembered feelings inside her chest were tiny explosions of joy.

But that was another woman's joy. Not hers. "That wasn't me."

"It was," he said. "You know it was. You and I, Emma, our souls have circled one another for a thousand years. Maybe more. Why, I canna know, but I mean to resolve things now, this time to move on."

Some inexplicable sense of loss came with those words. Could he be any clearer than that? He wanted to be done with her, even now. Wanted to be shed of whatever connection they'd formed in this in-between. For reasons still too unclear for her to understand, that broke her a little.

"D'ye see that moor, down there, near the cliffs?"

She looked to where he was pointing, to the giant rocks teetering on the edge of cliffs that were skyscraper tall. She nodded.

"I died there. Right there beside that bald rock."

Surprise and dread mixed inside her. "I suppose you're going to tell me how." She wasn't sure she wanted to know because he had some sort of accusatory look in his eye pointing it out. "And that your Violet, in some way, had something to do with it. Am I right?"

"We were to be married. The banns had already been read at the kirk. Only my death or yours would'a stopped it. I had just inherited my father's estate after my older brother, Edgar, was killed in a riding accident. I'd been named duke at my father's death a month earlier. Though it was my honor to carry on my father's name, carryin' his title wasna my choice, mind ye. I'd never set my sights on that. But my younger brother, Arthur, coveted that title. Wanted it for himself. He and I had never seen eye to eye on much, but he was my only livin' brother. I loved him."

Emma picked a stem of heather growing from a crack in the wall and ran the flowers between her fingers, imagining those two young men, pitted against one another in the name of wealth and title.

"I had a sister, too. Her name was Rowena. She was the youngest. Plain and small, with no experience with men. She was just seventeen when a wealthy British knob named Landon Sykes ruined her with scandal. He bragged of it in my hearing and Arthur's, sayin' she'd willingly gone to his bed. Rowena's reputation was destroyed. Her future would be ended right there without an answer."

Emma clenched her fists together in her lap. There was a buzzing in her hands, and she couldn't seem to stop it. "How terrible."

"Short of outright murder—which I preferred whole-heartedly—I challenged him to a duel to force him to retract his lies about Rowena. Arthur stepped up as my second, as angry as me about what had happened. Or so I thought."

"Wait, what's a 'second'?"

Patiently, he explained, "Someone—a friend, a broth-er—of your choosing to have yer back. To be sure nothing goes wrong. That the other party is no' planning to bring a load of lads to ambush you in case it does. They load and check the weapons."

"And after he did, Arthur looked me dead in the eye as he gave me my pistol. 'Kill him,' he told me, and for the first time, we agreed on something."

"Did Violet know what was about to happen? If it were me, I would have tried to stop you. I would have tried anything."

"Ye would've stopped nothin'. Let his lies stand? No." Connor lifted a handful of stone dust in his hand and tossed it to the wind, where it drifted past her. "But I haven't gotten to the good part yet."

"Go on, then."

"Ye see, Arthur misloaded my pistol. I pointed it at Sykes's heart, the hammer slammed shut. Nothing. I looked at Arthur, but he just shrugged with a look that told me it had been intentional just before Sykes's bullet found my chest. My blood was on his hands, every bit as much as the man who'd ruined our sister's good name. Ye see, he'd planned it all with Sykes, ruined our sister's name, watched me die. All so he could be named duke."

"Oh, Connor!" She reached for his hand. "How awful. What did Sykes get out of it?"

"He got you. Or Violet, as you like. Sykes leaned over me as I lay bleedin' out on the heather and made sure I knew Violet had already been his and would be his wife after I was gone."

"*What?*"

"And that is exactly what happened."

"No! I would never—!"

His expression flattened with self-righteousness as she put herself in Violet's shoes. "But she did. Which explains why she never came that day or even tried to comfort poor Rowena, who was her friend.

"And Rowena…she'd been just a pawn in my brother's scheme to get my father's title. And in exchange for this little plot of theirs, Sykes would steal away the woman he'd coveted, the woman I'd loved."

"Oh, Connor. How terrible." That story burrowed itself deep inside her, ripping at parts of her she'd never known were there. "But Violet—why would she—? How do you know she really—?"

"Because she did, in fact, marry the man who killed me,"

he snarled. "Bore him children. And lived wi' him till the day she died."

Emma leaned her head back against the stone. She had nothing to say to that except if it was true, he had every reason to hate Violet. The woman's betrayal still ate away at him after all this time. It explained so much. Somehow, he blamed her—Emma—for Violet's apparent infidelity. But that story made no sense to her, deep down—soul deep.

"And your brother? What happened to him?"

"He lived a short, unhappy life, childless wi' a woman who didna love him. His death," he added, "was slow and painful."

"You watched her? After?"

"No. I couldna watch. I learned of it later."

Emma blinked. "And this story about Violet's betrayal," she said carefully, "the story that came from Sykes's own mouth. You know this to be true?"

Connor turned her way with a curious expression. "I told you. She married the man and lived with him until her dying d—"

"Willingly? You're sure of this?"

His jaw worked as he tried to contain whatever he was thinking of her now.

"I'm only saying," she went on, "what if he lied about her? What if she had nothing to do with what happened? What if—"

"She knew of the duel. Arthur warned me she'd heard of

it and was bound to come. But she never did. Just as well, I suppose, that I didna have t' look her in the eye." He lifted his gaze to Emma. "Not till now."

Ouch. She stood and turned to look out over the moor. The cool breeze buffeted them gently. "I suppose you feel better now. Having me to blame for what happened?"

"I thought I would. But…" He leaned his elbows disconsolately against the stone. "No. Not much."

"I think you should consider the possibility that you were mistaken about her part in all that. That what they told you was a lie."

"What would you know about it?"

She shook her head at him. "Funny you should ask that after accusing me of sharing her soul all this time. Because I feel, deep down, there is more to her story than you know."

"I know all I need to know," he said, stubbornly.

"All you want to know, perhaps."

"*No.*" Connor pushed away from the stones and started down the ancient stairway, leaving her standing at the wall.

"I thought angels were all about forgiveness," she called after him, starting down the stairs. "You are seriously playing against type here."

He just kept stalking through the purple blossoms, leaving a small trail in his wake. She followed him but allowed some space to come between them. They didn't speak again until he'd reached the bottom of the hill where the trail forked between the road and the sea cliffs. There he turned on her.

"Dinna presume to judge me or what I've been doin' for the last…too many years—"

"I'm not—"

"—because I ken what I saw. I ken what happened."

"Fine."

"Right."

"Good. So, you should look no further than that bastard's word. That's fair."

He glared at her from beneath his brows. "Dinna twist my words, Emma."

"You mean Violet, don't you? That's what this whole thing was about, wasn't it? To prove your point about my being your faithless fiancée? Maybe you thought it would all come back to me—all my soul's transgressions—in a guilty rush, then I'd confess? And you could finally rid yourself of the bitterness that haunts you. But. Sorry. Not going to happen."

He reminded her suddenly of a boy, denied a baseball that he'd come close to catching.

"Connor," she went on, "in my soul, in my heart, I feel that something is wrong with that story. I think you know that, too."

"She never came." He shook his head. "She would'a come that day if it was a lie."

"You're right," Emma said, touching his hand. "But what we don't know is why she didn't come."

"Too late fer that. We canna know."

"Did you ever ask your friend, Elspeth, the record keeper, about her?"

His jaw grew rigid again. "No. 'Twas not somethin' I spoke of. Yer—well, yer—"

"I'm Violet, I know," she finished. "But maybe Elspeth could help you. Maybe she'd have information in her—"

"I told you, she's no guardian anymore. She's fallen."

"But you said she's got an uncanny memory. You know where she is. Right?"

He stared at her, considering. "I might. Come. It's time we get back."

Emma hesitated, taking in the beauty of the land around them. "It's hard to leave all this."

He didn't speak, but she could tell it was the same for him. Finally, with one last look, she took his hand. They left the country that had at once created and ruined him. The place that somehow lived in her soul.

AUBREY AND JACOB prowled through the wreckage of Emma's house, marveling at the thoroughness of the chaos. Nothing was left untouched. Filming the wreckage with her phone, Aubrey stared at the chaos in disbelief.

"You're not going to post that," Jacob said.

Aubrey shook her head. "Just documenting. But nobody

would believe this."

"Better to keep this part of it private. Who knows who watches those posts."

Aubrey sat on the edge of a chair, scraping her fingers through her hair. "I can't believe any of this is real. It's so crazy. Who would want to hurt Emma?"

Winston wound himself around her ankles. She picked up the cat, resting him across her shoulder. The cat purred loudly, happy to have familiar company.

"Do you see anything missing?" Jacob asked.

"I don't think so. My computer is broken," she said, pointing to it upside down on the floor, "but it's here. TVs, everything. Winston." She ruffled his fur with her fingertips. "*You* know who did this, don't you?" she said to the cat. "Can't you just tell us?"

Winston yawned, baring his teeth.

"Right. That about sizes things up. I know I totally forgot to feed him that night because I went directly to the hospital from our dinner with your parents. So, what kind of a robber feeds the cat on his way out anyway?"

"An animal lover?" Jacob suggested, topping off Winston's nearly full bowl of dry food.

"Sure. Probably rescues baby bunnies when he's not breaking and entering."

"Yeah, that is a mystery." Jacob lifted the scattered silverware drawer contents, putting the knives and forks on the counter. "For that matter, we don't know it was a guy.

Could have been a woman."

"And leave this mess?" She shook her head. "No, a woman would have been much more methodical. This was definitely a man's doing."

Jacob side-eyed her while filling a glass of water from the sink. He handed it to her. "I'm sorry. It's a lot."

She nodded, gulping down the water as a knock sounded at the back door. The two of them exchanged alarmed looks. "Who could that be?"

"Stay here," he told her and opened the back door.

The middle-aged woman at the back door was smiling timidly at him while peeking into the house behind him as she spoke.

"Oh, hello," she said, her voice scratchy as an old LP. "I'm Clarissa Meyer. I live next door. I saw you and Aubrey drive up. I just wanted to come by and check on how Emma's doing."

"It's okay, Jacob. Hi, Ms. Meyer."

"Oh, Aubrey!" she said, edging her way into the house past Jacob. "Oh, dear. I was so sorry to hear about your aunt. How is she? Oh! My! Look at this place!" She tsked with a sigh. "I saw the police in the neighborhood yesterday. I told them what I know. They interviewed me you see. How is Emma, dear?"

"Holding her own. Thanks for asking," Aubrey said. "What exactly did you tell the police?"

"Well, just that I heard some noises over here late that

night of the accident and there weren't any lights on. Not anything too loud, you understand. But loud enough to make me sit up in bed and wonder. But I just thought I should mind my own business, don't you know?"

Well, that would certainly be a first. Aubrey suppressed her grin. "Did you see anyone over here? Through the windows?"

"No. Not even a light. I thought maybe I had imagined the noise after a while. But I can see now that I hadn't."

"See anyone leave or any cars parked where they shouldn't be parked?" Jacob asked her.

At first, she shook her head, then said, "You know, now that you mention it, I'd forgotten this, but before I went to bed that night, I let my little dog, Reno, out for his nightly business. There was a car parked down the street that I didn't recognize. But that in itself isn't all that unusual. The odd part was that someone was just sitting in the driver's seat. Smoking. I caught the glow of a cigarette burning. It kind of gave me the creeps, but I just decided whoever it was was waiting for someone in a house down the street. I didn't think much more of it. I hurried Reno back in the house and went to bed."

"What kind of car was it?"

"Maybe...an SUV of some kind, I think. It was dark. You know how long we've been after the city for streetlights in this neighborhood? But if I had to guess, I'd say it was dark colored. Blue or black, maybe."

"So, you didn't tell the police about this car?"

"No. I'd forgotten all about it until just now. Did they take anything?" Clarissa asked. "I called a locksmith today. They changed all of my locks, got double bolts and bars for my sliders. This used to be a such safe neighborhood."

"Good idea," Aubrey said. "Thank you for stopping by. I'll tell Emma when she wakes that you were asking about her."

"Oh, thank you. If you need anything, Aubrey, just ask. Anytime. You're not staying here, are you? Mercy! What a mess. It'll take weeks to clean this up."

"No, I'm not staying here. Don't worry about me."

Clarissa patted her hand. "You take care now, dear."

After the woman left, Aubrey sat down on the edge of the couch, staring at the room.

"That's good information," Jacob said. "We should give that to the detectives."

Aubrey grabbed her wrist, trying to stop her hand from shaking. "What if I'd been here? Was he waiting for me to come home or waiting to see if I'd left already?"

The worry on Jacob's face deepened.

She reached for the necklace at her throat that she absently twiddled when she was stressed. She gasped. "My necklace! It's gone!"

"Your mom's peace necklace?"

"Yes! Did I drop it somewhere?" She crawled around the floor, looking under the jumble of stuff there.

"You're going to cut yourself on the broken glass." Jacob pulled her to her feet. "I didn't notice it before. I don't think you were wearing it."

"I always wear it." She hurried to her bedroom to look through the tangle of jewelry spread across her bed. "It's not here."

She couldn't think. It had belonged to her mother. One of the only things she'd left to her. It was a little nothing. A trinket. But it was special to her. And he was right. She never took it off.

Unless...

Unless she was getting a facial. Like she had two days ago.

Relief swamped her. "I must've taken it off at the spa. I must have left it there." She rubbed her forehead. "I can't even remember..."

He sat down beside her and rubbed her shoulders. "You're tired, Aub. We'll go there. We'll find it."

"No, wait. I...I didn't take it off at the spa. I remember now—Emma drove me, dropped me off, remember? You picked me up."

"And your necklace?"

"I took it off in Emma's car."

EMMA AND CONNOR stood at the entrance to the hospital,

but she balked at going in. He turned a curious look on her. "What?"

"I can't," she said. "Don't make me go back in there yet."

"Why not?"

"I need to be in the air, not in there." Trading the scents of Scottish Highlands for those of a hospital made her want to cry.

It had occurred to her, somewhere between that beautiful pile of ancient rocks in the Highlands and this asphalt-covered parking lot, that too much of her life had been wasted chasing something that she couldn't even hold. What she had done for the past nine years—sell homes, dreams to other people—was all well and good, until you stood back to look at your own life.

All the times she'd said no to a chance, backed away from an opportunity for happiness. All the personal sacrifice she'd made. And for what? Money? Security? Being alone?

Yes, she had Aubrey, but even that had not been by choice. Of course, she'd become like a mother to her niece, but only in exchange for losing Lizzy and her husband.

How brief life was. Her parents. Lizzy and Daniel. Even Connor, standing once on the brink of happiness with Violet only to have his world pulled out from under him. What was it that still haunted him from that life? It wasn't the loss of his considerable land or his title or even his faithless brother. It was the loss of the woman he'd loved. Her heart ached for him, even though she barely knew him.

Emma? Aubrey had told the police officer. *She was—is— married to her job.*

She supposed Aubrey was right. The truth was, she was a coward when it came to love. She'd never really risked what Connor had. Aside from Aaron, there had been two men with whom she'd dabbled in love. Stephen Black and Cody Burrows. Both years ago. Neither one substantial enough to earn more than a season of commitment from her in her early to mid-twenties. Stephen had wanted much more than she'd been willing to give him at that point, and the last time she'd seen Cody, he'd been straddling her best friend, India, in Emma's own bed, in the middle of an afternoon which she was, in hindsight, grateful she hadn't spent at the university library.

Maybe that was what had made a coward of her. Despite how other people saw her and the life she'd built, they didn't see the real her. Maybe she was no better than Connor's Violet. One thing to the world and another altogether deep down.

But something about that whole story he'd told her made her wonder. She had no reason to believe he could be wrong about it. He was an angel, after all. If anyone should know, he should. But something niggled at her. Something was off. Or maybe she just couldn't imagine hurting him the way Violet had. Or believe any part of her could have been responsible for such a thing.

"Where to?" he asked.

"A place I know." She took his hand, closed her eyes focused intensely on a place she knew, picturing herself there, feeling the grass beneath her feet. Moments later, they found themselves in Schooner's Bay, standing under a sprawling oak tree at the center of the park.

Connor stared at her in surprise. "How did you—?"

"Traveling's not that hard, is it?" she said. "You just have to think yourself somewhere. I just watched you do it."

"And yet," he said with a slow grin, "ye surprise me."

"Just keeping you on your toes."

The Fourth of July weekend was almost here, and as always, preparations were being made for the celebration that would take place here. There would be fireworks, raffles, bike decorating for the kids, a parade, and of course, the concert at night. It was as small-town America as you could get. She tugged him by the hand toward the gazebo at the center of the park.

All around them, volunteers were decorating the century-old gazebo with garlands and patriotic streamers. Fourth of Julys here had always been special. Emma rarely missed an opportunity to promote her company during this season, with park-bench ads and by cosponsoring the gazebo decorations. In fact, until Aubrey had come into her life to stay, she'd almost forgotten how much fun the Fourth could be. But once her niece had settled here, made friends, and become involved in this town, Emma had rarely missed a chance to mingle with friends, help with the decorations, or watch the fireworks from a blanket spread under the stars. Emma had forced herself to slow down in the past few years. To enjoy this celebration. Now she wondered if last year's fireworks show would be the memory Aubrey would store away because there might be no more with her.

But she hadn't come here to the park to torture herself with what-ifs. Instead, she wanted a moment of normalcy. To feel like she was still part of this world and all the people she knew.

There were Jen and Bob Bellows, an older couple who had lived down the street from her for years. They'd let her sell their home a few years back. After moving into a fifty-five-plus apartment, they'd never been happier. Never ones to let a good celebration pass them by, the two of them were wrapping crepe paper around a lamppost, sharing a beer with friends.

Near the amphitheater, where the concert would be held, Mayor Marks—Ronny to his close friends—and his wife, Linda, were doing a sound check for the sound system. Linda was trilling a silly song. The mayor was laughing while a half-dozen people who were lifting chairs off the flatbed truck nearby enjoyed their antics. At almost seventy-two, Ronny Marks had been mayor for four terms running, though he showed no signs of wanting to retire from politics. The community of Schooner's Bay seemed fine with that.

Lannie Walters, a newly widowed mother Emma knew

from high school, was there with her four young boys who were running around the park, largely unsupervised, as Lannie and Gabriella Harcourt, the event coordinator, checked off items on their clipboards, gossiping about the lead singer in the band set to perform at the celebration.

Life went on. Without her. Nothing had really changed, except her.

The smell of hot dogs and hamburgers barbecuing on Owen Baker's grill in support of all the volunteers made her stomach growl. She glanced at Connor, whose nose was also in the air, taking in the smell of food cooking.

"I bet you've never had a hot dog," she said.

"Aye. Ye'd be right about that," he said with a small grin.

"Or even a hamburger, I imagine."

"Not as if I've never smelled 'em before. But as ye know, 'tis a mortal pleasure to eat. 'Tis not somethin' we crave."

She nodded. "I'm craving it. Right now. I guess that means I'm still mortal. Sort of."

He smiled at her, that smile that made her feel all warm inside.

"All this," he said, pointing at the activity. "What's goin' on here?"

"Independence Day. It's a celebration…with fireworks and parades. Hot dogs. Very American."

He nodded. "Fireworks. I've seen 'em. They're bonnie."

"You like them?"

"The banger lights? Aye. You'll likely find a few guardians hangin' around t' watch the show."

"Banger lights?" She laughed. "Well, that's accurate at least. So, have you ever hung around this particular 'banger lights' show before? Would I have seen you and your…your wings if I'd looked hard enough?"

"No," he said, with a small smile. "Him, on the other hand…I would guess ye might've seen him."

She followed Connor's gaze to a man sitting on top of the gazebo—an impossible place to get to—cross-legged, watching one of Lannie's boys who had started climbing up a nearby elm tree. The man was dressed in a long dark coat, completely inappropriate for the warm weather. He looked vexed.

"Don't you do it, Nathan," he shouted out to Lannie's six-year-old son. "Don't. Do. It."

Not a single, solitary other person seemed to hear this man shouting at the boy, least of all Nathan himself as he started up the tree.

"Who is that?" she asked Connor, who had his eye on the boy.

"That's Henry," he said. "An old friend."

"You mean…he's a—?"

"Aye. A guardian, too."

Henry—a handsome youngish man with salt-and-pepper hair with a face and physique better suited to a Tom Ford runway—glanced down at Connor. He touched a finger to his forehead in salute. "Connor."

"Henry."

"This boy." Henry sighed, pointing to the hooligan who imagined himself Spider-Man. "He'll be the death of me yet."

Connor laughed. "A stubborn one, eh?"

"Downright defiant. *Nathan!*" he shouted again. "Think about your choices!"

Nathan was a born climber, a logic-defying risk-taker, and already he'd managed to clamber his way halfway up the gigantic tree near the gazebo. *Oh no.* Emma jerked a look at Lannie, who was still engrossed in gossip and not paying attention to her son's peril.

"Connor," she cried. "He could fall!"

"True. He might."

Emma stared at him in astonishment. "What kind of an answer is that from a guardian angel?"

"Ye dinna understand."

"That he's going to hurt himself? Badly?"

Connor sent her a testy look, continuing to do nothing. For his part, Henry sat on the gazebo, hands clasped atop his head in frustration, awaiting the inevitable as well.

Panic began creeping into her. "But isn't Henry his—?"

"Guardian? Aye, but he canna always interfere. 'Tis the boy's lesson to learn. Henry's tryin' to teach him."

"That it hurts to fall from a tree? That you can break your neck?"

"To listen to his inner voice. Henry, in this case."

"Connor!"

He slid a look at Lannie and shook his head.

That made no sense to her at all. If they wouldn't, she would! She raced to Lannie's side. "Look up, Lannie! Look at Nathan. He's way up in that tree. Look up!"

But Lannie couldn't hear her, of course. She went on chatting with Gabriella, laughing at something she said. Emma shoved a hand at her shoulder, but, naturally, her hand passed right through. Lannie scratched the spot as if a bug had landed on her.

Helplessly, she turned to Connor, who was watching the boy transfer from limb to fragile limb. Henry, whose wings were visible behind him, crouched now on the gazebo.

She gasped at the sound of a limb cracking, the sight of the boy tumbling, crashing down through the branches below him.

Beside her, Lannie finally caught sight of her son falling. For a horrifying instant, she froze. But by the time she was on her feet, she was too late. There was no way she could reach him in time.

Chapter Seven

I T WAS, INSTEAD, a fully visible Connor who stepped forward to hold out his arms to the boy. Nathan fell against him like a leaf finding the ground. Connor set him down safely on his feet. The slow-motion sensation of the fall sped up in a blink as the boy stared up at Connor's face and began to cry.

"Yer all right, then," he told the boy. "Dinna fear."

An instant later, Lannie was at the boy's side, scooping him into her arms, profusely thanking the stranger who had saved her son.

Connor waved off her thanks but gave the boy a man-to-man look of such tenderness, it nearly broke Emma's heart. In turn, Nathan sniffed and returned Connor's look with all the seriousness a six-year-old could muster and a solemn nod.

After Connor left them, making his way into a stand of trees to become himself again, Lannie could hardly contain her emotions. She sat down with the boy, right there on the grass with tears wetting her cheeks.

"Nathan," she cried, hugging him tightly. "When will

you learn? What would I do if I lost you, too?"

"Who was that man?" Gabriella asked, kneeling down beside her. "He was just here a second ago. Where'd he go?"

"I didn't even get his name," Lannie told her, hugging Nathan against her.

Emma turned to find Henry standing beside her.

"Which is why Connor doesn't do children," he said. "He's a softie. Lessons are sometimes painful."

She wasn't sure she liked this Henry character, but she was liking Connor more and more. "But aren't you supposed to protect children?"

He nodded. "Sometimes the hard lessons are the most valuable ones. It would only have been a broken arm this time. And a lesson learned." He looked her up and down. "So, who are you?"

"An in-betweener," Connor answered for her, joining them. "Henry, Emma. Emma, Henry."

Henry raised one brow in assessment. "Keeping your options open, eh? Can't decide? Stay or go?"

"No," she retorted. "I'm staying. I just need to wake up is all."

"Coma," Connor explained.

"Ah," Henry said a bit indifferently before perking up. "Oh, wait. I heard about this one. Isn't she your—"

"You'd better see to your boy there," Connor said, cutting him off and gesturing at Nathan, who was walking away with his mother. "He seems a bit at loose ends."

The twinkle in Henry's eye reappeared. "Right. Well. Good to see you again, Connor. It's been a while. Oh, did I forget to mention that Elspeth Aloysius asked after you?"

"She did?" Surprise lit his gray eyes.

"Last time I saw her in a little town called Leyton Grove, I believe. She seems quite happy there, all things considered. She and her mortal…can't think of his name—?"

"Sam," Connor supplied.

"Yes, Sam. Sam Wynter. Anyway, she said if I saw you to send her regards. So"—he clapped Connor on the shoulder—"regards. Also, to tell you she had something for you."

"For me? Unlikely."

"I couldn't say what it is she has. Just passing along a message. But after hearing about her in action at the Council, you'd do well not to ignore her. She's a force, that one. Not to be underestimated."

"Aye, she is that. Thanks, Henry."

"And, Connor, the next time you have the impulse to undo all my hard work with Nathan?" Henry said, starting after the boy and his mother. "Don't."

"No promises. But I think ye'll find that Nathan learned a fine lesson on this tree."

"Oh yeah? Exactly what did you tell him just then with that look?"

"That he'd do well to listen to his better angels. That would be you."

Henry laughed, spread his wings and bowed like a courtier, then disappeared down the trail after the boy.

Emma slipped her fingers in between Connor's, then smiled up at him. "Thank you. Lannie would have been lost if anything had happened to him."

He tightened his fingers around hers. "He's a good boy with a long life ahead of him. He'll be fine."

"And yet his guardian won't protect him and can't make him listen."

"Dinna think that Henry isna watchin' out for him. He is. 'Tis the bigger picture ye canna see. My interferin' likely would'a cost Nathan precious time had he not heard my intent."

"And did he? Hear you?"

"Oh, aye. He heard. Smart lad."

He perplexed her, almost as much as this whole situation she was in did. "Why did you act like you didn't care?"

He seemed surprised by that. "Ye dinna know me, Emma."

"You're right. I don't. But…what if I said I…I wanted to?"

Her words hung in the air between them. The look he gave her made her wish she could take it back. But she could still almost feel his kiss on her lips as his gaze fell to her mouth.

"Not how this works," he said a little too sharply, dismissing her question and tugging her along behind him across the grassy field.

In the next instant they were back at the hospital, hurrying down a corridor full of people.

"How *does* this work? All of this?" she asked, hurrying to keep up with his long-legged strides as she avoided gurneys in the hallway. "And why are we paired up here in the in-between? Can you answer me that? I mean, I could have gotten someone...anyone else. Henry or...or anyone. But no. I got you. And you're stuck here with me. Why?"

His jaw went ridged again. "I was assigned—"

"I know. But why?" She wasn't sure why she needed to know this, but suddenly, it seemed important.

He turned back to her. "What does it matter? It just is."

"It matters to me."

"Dinna think too hard on it, Emma. 'Tis a temporary thing, and sooner or later, it will be over and done. If it means I can let ye go once and for all, then it's all for the good."

"Ah," she said quietly, feeling his words with unexpected sharpness. "I wonder how that works, though? Since I'm not her, there's nothing I can do to change your past with her."

The answer to that question seemed as far away as she did right now from the life she'd lived only two days ago. The one where she'd been so caught up trying to fix everyone else's life she'd forgotten about her own.

Connor let go of her hand as they reached her ICU room. The glass doors were closed, but to Emma and Connor, they were no barrier. There were nurses and doctors scurrying around between rooms. It wasn't until they were inside hers that Emma gasped at the sight of her empty bed. The sheets were turned down, all the machines were unhooked and silent.

That other Emma was...*gone.*

"Oh my..." She felt like she might faint. "Am I dead?"

AUBREY AND JACOB had stopped at the impound lot to search Emma's wrecked car, unsuccessfully, for her necklace before heading to the police station to speak to the detective in charge of Emma's case.

Detective Charmbers had written down their information Emma's neighbor, Clarissa, had given them about the SUV parked nearby the night of Emma's accident. Now he was taking an unrelated call as they sat across from him. Aubrey slid a look at Jacob.

Charmbers had said he'd interviewed a half-dozen neighbors the day after the break-in, including Clarissa, who had failed to mention the SUV. No one else had noticed the unfamiliar car, and with no license plate or other solid identifying factors, they had no way to track down the driver who might or might not have had anything to do with their break-in. At this point, he'd said, that car's involvement in the break-in was pure conjecture.

Aubrey bit her tongue, knowing she needed the police's

cooperation if nothing else. But she hadn't spent her Friday nights pre-Jacob watching *Dateline* episodes for nothing. Investigations like this took months, sometimes years to uncover truths.

Detective Charmbers hung up the phone, folded his arms, and leaned back in his chair. "We did speak to your aunt's ex"—he checked his notes—"Drake Lasserman, Esquire. Turns out he has an airtight alibi for that night. We also checked out his car. No damage. We have managed to narrow down the focus from the debris found on the road. It came from a 2016 Explorer SUV. Black. Lasserman's car was a Mercedes SUV. Silver."

"I never thought Drake could have...would have..." Frustrated, she stood, pacing in the small office. "Can you at least check to see if the necklace I mentioned might be in your evidence room?" she asked. "Maybe it was collected at the scene?"

He'd checked. It wasn't. Even if it was, it would be considered evidence and not accessible to her.

"You say you left it in the car the night of the incident?" he asked.

"I had an unexpected thing come up. Emma was covering for me. I went to the spa for a quick facial. Jacob picked me up from there. Emma went to the meeting. I specifically left the necklace in the console of her car so I wouldn't lose it. It's not valuable. It's just sentimental."

Charmbers rubbed his jaw. "So," he said, "if not for this

unexpected 'thing' you say had come up at the last minute—"

"Dinner with Jacob's parents who'd surprised us by coming to town."

"Right. But if not for that, it would have been you driving down that road that night. Not your aunt?"

"Well," she answered. "Yes." She'd been over this scenario in her head a hundred times but couldn't make sense of it.

The detective absorbed that for a moment, steepling his fingers together. "This appointment. It would have been on the books for a while? At your office?"

"On the office calendar, where all our appointments land. So that everyone knows where we're supposed to be at any given time." If she looked right now, her name would still be written under that appointment, not Emma's.

Her eyes suddenly stung with dampness. If it was supposed to be her, then whoever had driven Emma's car off the road had mistaken her aunt for her.

Jacob took her hand. "Aubrey's car's been in the shop for a couple of days. She's been sharing Emma's car."

"So, here's a question for you. Can you think of anyone who might want to hurt you, Ms. Wilhelm?" Charmbers leaned forward, hands folded on his desk. "Because if Ms. James was somehow mistaken for you, then maybe we've been staring up the wrong tree for a motive."

EMMA WAS NOT dead. Not yet anyway.

In fact, she was in the OR, having the surgery to mend her broken leg which, apparently, they'd been waiting to do until her condition had stabilized. Or stabilized enough to withstand surgery.

Connor stood to one side of the operating table watching the surgeon work on the other Emma. Beside him, his Emma turned her face away and focused on the music piping through the room, an upbeat mix of pop songs, apparently chosen by the surgeon. While the anesthesiologist kept an eye on her oxygen levels, the surgeon placed pins in her shin as he teased his surgical nurse about her football-player fiancé.

"If you can't invite us to the wedding, Gabi," the surgeon told her, "at least get us a couple of autographed pictures. You know I'm a fan of Washington football. I'll get mine framed and hang it right there on that wall over there."

"Oh, okay," Gabi quipped. "I'll make sure to do that so I can feel Kelvin watching me at work twenty-four seven."

Laughter rippled through the room. Gabi blushed behind her mask. "You don't see me all up in his business on the field. So, if you don't mind, please keep that autographed photo in your own screening room, Doctor."

"Fair enough." The surgeon chuckled. "But if I got you a football for him to—"

The nurse gave him the evil eye.

"Okay, okay," he said, still laughing. "Pin, please."

Feeling slightly offended by their lighthearted banter, Emma grimaced. "This is why they put you out during surgery," she told Connor. "So that you don't have to hear how much fun your surgeon is having patching you up."

As they teased one another under the hot lights, they worked with quick efficiency and, no doubt, immense skill. Though to Emma, they might as well have been working on an automobile or a broken fax machine, not a human being who genuinely hoped to use that leg again one day.

Emma caught Connor's look as he watched her. "'Tis no' personal. They mean nothing by it. 'Tis just their way. If they allowed themselves to get too close, they couldn't do what they do."

"And you have personal experience with twenty-first century surgeons, do you?"

"Ye forget, their thoughts are no' private from me. As a guardian, I've taken my share of them. They are only human, with all the frailties that come with the title."

"Right," she said, forcing away the sadness that had just descended on her. "*Grey's Anatomy* is proof of that."

"Grey's what?"

Emma rubbed her temples, leaning against Connor's strong shoulder. "I'm feeling a little nauseous right now. Can we get out of here, please?"

His hand stroked her arm with an unexpected gentleness, one that made her want to lean into him for comfort. "You go, lass. I'll stay here a bit and keep an eye."

Keep an eye?

The icy fear that had been hovering beneath her skin since the accident surfaced again. Did he know something she didn't know? The nausea at the back of her throat was the very thing she'd steadfastly refused to look at or completely acknowledge. She stood on some precipice, somewhere between living and not living. The real pain was behind her. Death, per se, was not what she feared. It was the leaving behind. That's what she feared. All the people she loved. All the things she'd left undone. All the bravery she'd never mustered. The hope she'd relinquished time and time again that her life could be everything she'd wanted it to be. Now perhaps those choices were out of her hands. Perhaps they'd already been made for her and this…this in-between place was simply to allow her to get used to the idea.

But it was more than that. It was this moment in time with Connor, to know him, to help him, maybe, in letting go of…her? It was what he wanted. It seemed the least she could do for him, considering she'd clearly not learned the lessons she'd been sent here for.

But even separating herself from him now, walking down the hospital corridor without him, she felt exposed. Alone. Bereft without him at her side. That couldn't be good.

Her feelings for him had taken a shift somewhere between showing her his wings and catching Nathan in his arms. For all his gruff bitterness toward Violet, there was another part of him that was equally gentle and kind. The way he looked at her, cared for her. Kissed her.

"Dinna think I haven't imagined this every day for centuries. Dinna think I haven't wanted to taste ye again. And now I have."

Even now, she felt those words cut her. She'd wanted him to kiss her. Wanted to taste him, too. To feel what his Violet must have felt in his arms. Had he imagined that kiss all these years? Had it lived up to his memories? She supposed not since he hadn't kissed her again. Either way this went, he would go his way and she would go hers. But what if that kind of thinking was exactly what she regretted most about her life? What if chances were simply out there in the universe, waiting for us to take them?

Emma shook her head as she passed people in the hallway. But seriously, how screwed up did the universe have to be to send her soul mate to her as an angel?

Aubrey and Jacob were in the waiting room. Aubrey was pacing around the chairs.

It was obvious she was upset. At first, Emma thought it was because of her surgery. But Jacob walked up beside her. "You can't blame yourself," he told Aubrey. "There's nothing you could have done to change things," he said, pulling her up against him. "I'm glad it wasn't you. I don't know what I'd do if it had been you."

Emma moved nearer, confused by this.

"I'm younger than her," Aubrey argued. "Maybe I would have fared better in the accident. I mean, Emma's almost middle-aged."

"Hey! I'm only thirty-three!" Emma protested. But what was Aubrey talking about? What should she have known? Why on earth would she want to trade places?

"Don't do that to yourself," Jacob told her. "We just have to figure out who it was that hit Emma and how they knew she—or you—would be on that road that night."

"It's the 'why' I don't get. Why would anyone want to hurt either of us? What were they looking for?"

"I don't want to sound nuts," Jacob said, "but the only thing that seems to be missing in all this is your necklace."

"That's... No." She shook her head. "I told you. My mom gave it to me as a little good-luck charm right before she...before she and my dad went missing. I didn't even get it in the mail until after we heard about their disappearance. That necklace was only special to me. No one else could possibly want it. Certainly no one would try to kill me for it. It's probably just somewhere out in the field where the accident happened. Emma did flip the car twice. It could have landed anywhere."

Emma squeezed her eyes shut as fleeting snippets of memory of that night suddenly crashed through her: the grassy ditch careening toward her in the cone of her headlights; the rain-slicked blacktop; the washing-machine spin cycle she'd found herself in; and, most importantly, a shadowy figure leaning over her through her car window, tugging at her clothes.

Emma spun wide-eyed to find Connor walking toward her.

"What?" he asked her with a frown.

"I remember."

AS EMMA RELAYED her memories of how the accident happened, Connor glanced down at the dial on his wrist: +22 percent. Now they were getting somewhere. If luck was with him, he'd get out of this assignment with Emma unscathed and move on to what he was supposed to be doing. Forget that the feelings she was stirring in him had no place to go. Or his very un-Celestial impulse to pull her against him, touch her. and protect her from whatever pain she was about to encounter, be that a continuation of her life or…her death.

"That other car kept bumping mine from behind. I was so scared," Emma said, shaken by the memory. "Maybe he wanted me to pull over, but there was zero chance of that happening. But then—"

"Did ye get a good look at the driver?"

She shook her head. "Only in the rearview mirror, but their headlights were in my eyes and it was pitch dark."

"If ye saw them again?"

"I don't know."

"But ye remember someone leanin' over ye in the car?

Do ye remember him speakin' to ye? Sayin' anything?"

"Not...I can't really remember that. I couldn't make out their face, but something was in my eyes. Blood, I suppose." She shook her head. "That's all until everything went black. The next thing I knew, I was standing on that hillside in the rain. It was like I was...feeling so separate from the woman in the car. From me. And everything was...blank."

Connor nodded, remembering. "So, we're no closer."

"The detective was right. It was an SUV. But that doesn't help things, does it?" She glanced around the waiting room, at Aubrey and Jacob, huddled together on the couch waiting for word of her surgery. "If Jacob is right about the necklace...if that's what they want, which I can't imagine, maybe it's somehow tied into Lizzy and Daniel's world. Their deaths? That old necklace was just a piece of costume jewelry from Lizzy. She's worn it since college, I think."

Connor pulled the necklace from his pocket where he'd stuffed it after finding it at the scene of the accident.

"You kept it?" she asked, reaching for the necklace. But of course, she couldn't hold it. Frustrated, she flopped down onto a lounge sofa, sprawling backward. "Ugh. This is impossible."

He fingered the green jewel set in the bottom of the peace symbol. It was a large, almost gaudy piece of green glass, cut like a teardrop that fit perfectly into the bottom third of the peace symbol. "What about this piece of—is it cut glass?"

"Probably. I don't remember it specifically from back in the day. But an emerald was Lizzy's birthstone—May—so she must have added that at some point. I mean, obviously, it's fake, but—"

"What if it's not?"

Emma frowned. "It's...huge. It couldn't be real. We always assumed—"

"Maybe you shouldn't."

Emma sat up. "Do you think it could be—?"

"They were treasure hunters, you said, your sister and brother-in-law. What do you know about their passing?"

Emma seemed unable to shutter the pain in her expression. "Only that their boat was found abandoned, like a ghost ship, off the coast of Florida. It was found floating somewhere in the Bermuda Triangle. We were never sure what happened to them. Whether they were pirated and murdered or what happened. They were veteran sailors. But we'll never know."

Connor stared at the square of sunlight pouring through the window at the end of the hall. "We might be able to find out."

"What? How?"

He pocketed the necklace again, nodding toward the pair of detectives and an officer in uniform walking toward Aubrey and Jacob, just as the surgeon from Emma's surgery walked into the waiting room from the other door.

Ignoring the officers, Aubrey jumped up to talk to the

surgeon. "Is she—?"

"She did well. As well as could be expected," said the surgeon, who'd only minutes ago been joking about his nurse's wedding. Emma had to admit, without his mask, he was quite handsome. "We set her leg, inserting plates and screws to secure the bone. It should heal well. And if—*when* she wakes up, she'll have to go through some rehab for it. But I've seen worse."

Aubrey brushed away a tear. "Thank you for saying that. Thank you for believing she will wake up and walk again."

"I always have hope for my patients. Your aunt is young and strong. She's made it this far. She'll be in recovery for a bit, then you can see her again." He patted Aubrey's hand, and she thanked him.

She hugged Jacob, relief evident in her tears. "You should go," she told him. "I'll stay here. You can't miss any more work."

"I don't want to leave you alone."

"I'll be fine. I'm surrounded by people here. Nothing will happen. You can't lose your job over this. Please. Go."

Jacob checked his phone and the list of missed calls. "Only if you promise to stay here. At the hospital. I'll come get you later when I'm finished at work. They're getting slammed on the Trinity case."

"I know. Go. I'll stay here. Promise," Aubrey told him.

He kissed her goodbye and headed off toward the exit. Aubrey slumped back down onto a chair in the waiting room, combing her fingers through her hair.

Emma sat down on the chair beside her. "It's going to be okay, Aubrey. No matter what. It's going to be okay. You'll see."

But both she and Connor knew that was a big white lie. She still didn't know which way this would go. Maybe Connor did, but he wasn't telling her. Did other people who landed in the in-between stay here long? Was she minutes away from waking up? Or going in the other direction? Was it her time or not? How would she know?

She'd always believed that when it was your time, it was just your time. But it certainly felt like some cosmic mistake had been made in her case. That, first of all, the accident had possibly only happened because they'd thought she was Aubrey. Which was terrifying. So, whose fate was at play here? Hers? Or Aubrey's? She couldn't even consider anything happening to Aubrey. She simply wouldn't allow it.

She shook her head, wanting to hug her niece. If only she could get to the bottom of all this.

"Let's go, then," Connor said, reaching for her hand.

"Go where?"

"To the bottom of it all," he said with a wink.

"You *have* to stop doing that," she told him.

"Aye, right."

"I'm serious."

"I know," he said, pulling her up from the chair.

She sent a look back at her niece. "But what about…"

"Dinna worry. She'll be safe. This willna take long."

Confused, Emma stopped resisting. For reasons she couldn't begin to fathom, when he put his hand in hers, curled his fingers around hers, she trusted him.

They started down the corridor together. In the next instant, they were in another place altogether. A pretty, green place, with a lake beside it that smelled of summer and of the fragrant pines bending in the July breeze. There was a gabled house with a wide, screened porch in the back, pretty as a picture with a flower garden surrounding it. A stunning woman with blond hair was sitting in an Adirondack glider on the lawn with an infant snuggled against her shoulder in the warm sun. There was a Fourth of July banner strung across the front of the porch with little handmade red, white, and blue triangles.

Emma tightened her fingers around Connor's. The look on his face reminded her of a boy on the first day of school—at once excited and nervous.

"Where are we?" Emma asked Connor.

"Leyton Grove." He pointed to the woman in the glider. "And she's an old friend of mine."

Chapter Eight

EMMA FROWNED. AN old friend? What exactly did that mean? He'd been an angel for centuries. How old could she be?

The woman, who was definitely not an angel, was waving to a sailboat doing maneuvers offshore on the sprawling lake, catching the wind in its sails. It reminded her of a boat her father had owned for a few years that he'd sailed on the ocean. She'd been on it many times, and the sight brought a rush of memory and emotion. This boat was pristine looking, made of wood. From here, Emma could make out a man and a young girl who was helping with the rigging. Connor was watching the boat, too, smiling at the sight.

The woman in the Adirondack chair jumped to her feet, shocked and happy to see Connor, who had materialized before her.

"Well, if it isn't my favorite Scotsman," she said, striding toward him.

"Elspeth," he said, reaching out to hug her. "And who's this wee bairn?" He peeked behind the blanket in her arms. A small perfect little face appeared and scrunched in a yawn.

A tuft of wispy blonde hair covered the crown of her head.

"This is Anika Noel, our little girl. Sam's and mine. Molly's, too, of course." She blushed as she spoke.

"I hadn't heard. She's…well, she's bonnie, Elle. *Meal do naidheachd.* Congratulations."

"Thanks," she said, beaming. "We couldn't be happier."

Elspeth. Elle. She had the look about her of a woman who was perfectly herself, right with her world. Happy. Emma remembered then hearing about her, twice now. Connor had told her that she'd been one of them—a guardian—before she'd quit to be with the man she'd fallen in love with, Sam Wynter, who was apparently the one steering that boat out on the lake. Curious, Emma wanted a better look at the man who'd changed an angel's mind.

But if she ever got to tell anyone she'd been with two Celestial beings (one fallen) chatting away a few hundred miles from the bed she lay in, surely no one would believe her. She wasn't sure if she believed it herself.

"I suppose this is what Henry meant when he said you had something for me? This little surprise?" Connor said to Elle about the baby.

"Well, she was a surprise, but not the one I meant Henry to mention to you. But first, are you going to introduce me to your lovely friend? Or will you make me do that myself?"

Emma said, "You can see me? But I thought—" She sent a confused look at Connor, who nodded at her. Reaching out a hand to Elspeth before remembering her own limitations, she said, "I'm Emma."

"She's...in-betweener," Connor explained with a look brimming with subtext.

"Yes," Elspeth said with a smile. "Very nice to meet you, Emma."

"Same. It's...so beautiful here. And she's adorable, little Anika."

"Thanks. And we do love it here. That's Sam out on the boat and our daughter, Molly. Now that Sam has finished building that thing, you can't keep them out of it. But I'm kind of glad I stayed ashore today. I had a feeling I might see you soon."

"Did ye, now?"

"Come, sit down. We have a lot to discuss."

They sat in the Adirondack chairs positioned around a fire pit. It was too warm for a fire, but the fragrance drifting from the cold ashes in the pit reminded Emma of campfires as a child with s'mores and roasted hot dogs. All such simple human pleasures. She wondered if she'd ever have them again.

And babies.

Gazing at Anika, who had started to fuss, it struck her that even a fallen angel could have a baby. Yet that blessing had also eluded Emma herself in this life. Maybe now it was truly too late.

Elle found a pacifier and pressed it against the baby's perfect, heart-shaped mouth. Anika stopped fussing and settled back to sleep.

"I hear big things are about to happen for you, Connor, At least, that's the rumor."

"Y'are surprisingly well informed for a reformed Celestial."

"I do have my connections," she replied with a grin. "Henry, for one. He always keeps a finger on the pulse of things."

"More like an ear to the ground. But aye, it seems I'm going t' make the Council after all. After I'm finished here."

He said, as if I'm not sitting right beside him. Emma sank down a little in her chair.

"Congratulations to you!" Elspeth squeezed his hand. "That's wonderful. It's what you've always wanted. Right?"

He flicked an unreadable look at Emma. "Aye. It is."

Emma kept quiet, but her head spun with questions she knew she had no business asking. When exactly would he be finished here? When she, what, gave up the ghost? Bit the bullet? Kicked the bucket? Or when she returned to her real life and left this incomprehensible substitute for a life behind?

"So, you've come because Henry sent you? Or for some other reason?" Elle asked, rubbing her baby's back, a motion that seemed as natural to her as breathing.

"Your news first," Connor said.

She shifted the sleeping baby to her other shoulder. "Okay, but…" She glanced at Emma questioningly.

"'Tis all right," he assured her. "Say what you will."

From her diaper bag, she pulled a book—small tome that looked quite old. "I've kept it with me, hoping I'd see you one day soon." She handed it to him. "You know Iris."

He nodded.

"Her life here for the last forty years was as a librarian. Anything you wanted to find, she could find it. Out of curiosity one day, I asked her to go looking for you."

"Me?" A frown pulled at Connor's brow.

"Well, your history. I'm a little nosy that way."

"And?"

"She came across this little book. It was published in the mid-eighteen hundreds by a man named Ezra Bean, who was enthralled with the Scottish patriarchy and what happened to it after the Battle of Culloden."

"Culloden was long before my time."

"I know. That was interesting, but not as interesting as the chapter about your family."

"*My* family?" he said with a humorless chuckle. "You mean that pit of traitorous vipers, don't you?"

"Your brother, no doubt. But in his research, Mr. Bean came across some diary entries that hadn't seen the light of day for over fifty years."

"A diary? Whose?"

"Apparently," she said, glancing at Emma, "it belonged to Violet."

The color left Connor's handsome face, and his jaw went

rigid.

"Apparently," Emma put in, "I *am* Violet. If such things are to be believed."

Elspeth's expression softened. "I know. I heard that, too, from Marguerite."

Connor shot to his feet. "Oh, for the love of—Does everyone know my business but me?"

Emma stared at the book with the strangest feeling tugging at her. Her words, written two hundred odd years before, by her alter ego. But this validated everything he had told her about the woman he'd once loved, the one who'd broken his heart.

"You should read it," Elspeth told him. "This one section anyway. Though Bean has a nineteenth-century take on everything she said, I think those entries were meant for you."

"I don't want to read it," he told her.

"Well, *I* want to read it," Emma piped in. "After all, I wrote it. Isn't that the going theory?"

Connor sent her a grouchy side-eye. "And how, exactly, will that work, Emma? Shall I turn the pages for you? Hold the book at eye level for ye so ye can take in all the juicy scandal of it? So ye can read all your love letters to your devil of a husband?"

"That's hardly fair," Emma argued. "You can't be mad at me because I'm trying to sort out what you clearly don't want to."

"She has a point," Elspeth agreed, lowering the babe to cradle her in one arm.

He scowled at her. "Oh, aye. You, too?"

She pushed the book in his direction. "Just read the excerpt, Connor. I think you'll find it enlightening. At the very least clarifying."

"What?" he asked. "*Now?*"

"Not the whole book. I marked the pages," Elspeth encouraged.

Reluctantly, he took the small book, staring down at it as if it might contain one of those vipers he'd mentioned. "Fine. But it won't change a thing."

Elspeth smiled sweetly at him but kept her thoughts to herself.

Scanning the yard with a scowl, he headed down to the dock on the water to read in private.

Elspeth turned to Emma. "I should apologize for him, but I won't. He can be cranky, but his heart is good. He's one of my favorites."

Yes, that she understood. He was hers as well. Emma had settled her gaze on him already, watching the way he moved—with duke-ish confidence—as he stalked off to the water, oozing sexy power without even trying. He must have been something in life. She would really have liked to have seen that.

Heat climbed, unbidden, through her, as it did so often when she was near him or watching him or thinking of him.

Was it specifically against the universe's rules to covet an angel? To imagine that powerful body of his entwined with hers? To picture him holding her, touching her, kissing her without all the baggage he carried around in his soul?

And how foolish was she to imagine such things? With an angel, whose aspirations were for some otherworldly position she couldn't even fathom. Superbly foolish, that's what.

"He's not without his charm," Emma managed to say. "I do have a theory about Violet, though. One he doesn't share. I'm not sure whatever that book says will make any difference in how he feels about her. Or me."

"Oh, I don't know," Elspeth said cryptically. "You could be wrong."

She exhaled a laugh. "It wouldn't be the first time."

"I must admit, I can see now why Connor has been so obsessed with Violet all these centuries. I hear you're the spitting image of her. You're quite stunning, you know."

Surprised at her words, Emma said, "That's very kind of you to say." She lifted her one bare foot up and wiggled her toes. "Despite the fact that I've come to visit a perfect stranger half-shoeless?"

"Despite that fact," Elspeth agreed, laughing. "I know you must be feeling a bit—very—torn right now, being so displaced. I hope Connor's been of some comfort to you."

Emma turned to him. "Yes. He has. Mostly against his will. But yes."

"He's very private. In fact, until I read that book that Iris found, I didn't know much about his history, either. I knew there was someone named Violet in his past. He kept the details mostly to himself. But there was always something percolating under the surface with him. Something that has kept him from moving on. That something is you, of course."

"I am not Violet. But sometimes…sometimes for just a moment, I feel her. I remember her."

"Soul memory is a thing," Elspeth acknowledged. "I think you're both unavoidably entwined together in each other's destinies. I'll tell you a secret. I felt that way about Sam. Though I couldn't say why, I just knew he was meant to be mine and I was meant to be his. That's all there was to it."

"Well, I'm afraid Connor doesn't feel that way about me at all. Even if he did, we're from different worlds now. He has other plans."

Elspeth sent her a sympathetic look.

"But can I ask you a question?" Emma pressed.

"Of course."

"You're…human now, right? Yet you can see me and Connor. But no one else can see us."

Elspeth laughed again, rocking Anika in the glider. "I can see how that would be confusing. I must admit, explaining this to a mortal who is in the in-between is a first for me. But yes, I was a Celestial once. But I petitioned the Council to allow me to fall. To be human, but not through rebirth. Because I knew I had to be with Sam and Molly. But you see, when humans and angels interact on Earth, as Sam and I did when I was here on a mingle, they forget us as soon as we return to the Celestial world."

"But you and Sam—?"

"Yes, that's complicated, but it all worked out for us. Sam knows my past now. I've told him. But still, he's mortal. He can't see Connor and certainly not you, as I can. As I always will be able to. At least in this lifetime."

"So, you're saying I'll forget Connor if I wake up from this…accident?"

"It's hard to say. The in-between has different rules. You're not exactly human in this form, and your interaction is altogether different. Your memories of this time—if you survive—might survive as well."

If you survive…

Emma turned to look at Connor, who was poring over the book Elspeth had given him, trying to imagine forgetting all about the times his fingers had curled around hers or the way she'd caught him watching her when he hadn't thought she'd seen—those gray-blue eyes of his probing her soul. Or forgetting that ancient ruin in Scotland where he'd taken her. Or the kiss they'd shared. Impossible to think all of this could be erased from her memory by simply waking, the way a dream might disappear on the tip of one's tongue or the way clouds vanished into the vast blue without a trace.

But maybe there was hope at least that she would remember him. At the very least, she might be left with that.

"Now," Elspeth said finally. "I know you've come about something else. So let's talk for a moment about your sister, Lizzy."

CONNOR SAT ON the sun-warmed deck, legs folded, with the book in his hands, turning pages he never thought he'd turn, reading words he never imagined he'd hear. Violet's words.

14 July 1802

My dearest,

Can one love better than I? Can one man be more perfect than mine? I think 'tis not possible to be happier than I am this very morning!! Even my parents are unaware of our bonds, for we mean to surprise them. We shall tell them together this Sunday's eve, at the gathering at our home for supper. The promise you gave me at our ruins shall hold me until then! Oh, my heart. You love me!

Connor felt emotion clog his throat. How young she sounded. How hopeful. Yet Ezra Bean's commentary that followed demeaned her hopefulness as girlish fantasy. He went on to describe Violet's father, Lord Gray, as a desperate man who was surprisingly deep in debt from gambling, games that had included the elite of the town, mentioning several men, including Landon Sykes. This he hadn't known. Bean noted that his debts were mysteriously discharged soon after Violet's subsequent marriage to Sykes. A chill chased across his skin. Could Violet have known about this? But what had never made sense to him was that as her husband, Connor himself would have looked after her family. Her father must have known that.

The journal went on:

16 July 1802

What madness is this? How could this happen? Rowena ruined? I do not believe a word of it. Father is furious and forbidding me to see her or you. He will not listen to reason. He will not say why. Is it the scandal he's afeared will ruin me, too? But I am ruined without you. Ruined. Do not go tomorrow. I beg you—if God hears me—do not meet him in that field.

Arthur, protect him. There is something wrong with all this.

Connor scowled. Might as well have spit in the wind, for all the good that prayer did.

17 July 1802

I cannot breathe! The sun is breaking. What horror might come at first light? I am locked in my room to prevent me from coming to you. I'd climb out the win-

*dow, but my father has perched himself below to keep
me here. A prisoner! I hate him today, God forgive me.
But if anything befalls you, my love, I swear, my father
will never know my forgiveness.*

And we all know what happened next, he thought.

Connor skimmed down the page and a handful of para-
graphs Bean had written pragmatically about Connor's death
and how Arthur had surprisingly refused to honor his late
brother's promise to marry Violet. To take her as a bride in
his stead. It would have been the honorable thing to do, but
then, Arthur hadn't owned an honorable bone in his body.

It was, instead, Landon Sykes she would marry, an unexpected windfall for the family in dire need of one. There was
a copy of the banns, read in the parish kirk three Sundays in
a row, to announce their engagement.

Oh, that he could have been there in the parish to object
to that unholy union.

28 July 1802

*I cannot see ahead. I cannot. If Father forces me to do
this thing, I'll surely die of fury. For I ken now what
Landon Sykes and your brother did. What they both did
to you. May they rot in hell.*

Connor went hot then cold by turns. Guilt washed over
him.

He'd been wrong. Dead wrong that she'd been a part of

it. Now, remembering that treachery, how he'd blamed her for marrying Sykes, he could see that he'd been blinded to it before. Somehow, she'd put the pieces together about their plot. Reading her words felt as if she'd reached across the centuries to speak to him. All this time, he'd been wrong. Horribly, unjustifiably wrong. It wouldn't have taken Arthur long to take his place as heir after Connor's death. Or to revel in his newfound rank. Had he even feigned grief for his brother?

Ezra Bean called Violet's comments "hysteria" and a typical example of a willful daughter resisting her duty. A man of his times, Bean gave no credit to a woman's choice. But who was Connor to cast aspersions? He had been no better.

12 August 1802

'Tis done. Against my will. Better that piece of lead should have found my breast instead of yours that day, my love. But my life is over all the same. My father has sold me to your murderer for the price of a dowry and a promise of a generous yearly stipend. I bit the bastard and drew blood when he tried to kiss me. I will kill him if he touches me. I swear it.

Connor read several more entries of her misery, her threats on Sykes's life. But then all entries stopped for almost two years, when Bean noted the next two entries were from a new journal altogether.

16 May 1804

It infuriates him that I never say his name. But it makes me oddly happy to see him so. No use in explaining why he lives grand and my soul dies, slowly, day by day. Ye must know why. I long hoped he would end me. But he got me with child instead. Now when he comes to me at night, I close my eyes tight and think of ye. If I didn't, I would spend the rest of my days in cell away from my wee bairns. Or hanged, more like, for his death. If it wasn't for my son, Joseph, and my daughter, Eliza, I'd welcome my own death. I promise you that.

23 November 1805

Where are you, my love? I look up at the night sky and imagine you seeing those same stars from above. I miss your hands on mine. Your mouth on mine. I miss the kindness in your eyes. I must hide this diary, for I am with child again. He will hurt me if he finds this book, but I canna risk this child. His child. I should hate it, but I will not. I am not a real woman except for them. Only a smudge of ash on the wall of my room. A shadow. But the children make me remember you and what we could've been. And every day, I pretend they are yours.

He put the book down, staring into the water at the minnows swimming there amongst the clouds dancing across the water. He could not bear to read more. Couldn't bear all the bitterness he'd held onto for so many years, when she'd suffered so at the hands of the man who'd killed him. How could he have imagined she'd gone willingly to Sykes? Or borne him children with an open heart? Connor's own heart twisted. The fault wasn't in her but in him. He'd been but a shell of the man he'd once been. Half here and half there.

The fragrance of the crisp water, the sky, sharply blue against the green trees, it all reminded him of things he'd forgot, the simple pleasures of the mortal world, suddenly free from the shadow of his bitterness.

In all the time he'd been a Celestial, he'd stuffed his past into a pocket and kept it in the dark where it had safely festered for far too long. Why hadn't he pushed for answers? Why hadn't he sought her out sooner? Or imagined he'd gotten it all wrong about Violet? His brother he'd written off long ago, but Violet… He'd blamed her all these years for something he'd made up in his head. If he could talk to her now, to Violet, what would his excuse be? That his love for her had not been enough to guess the truth? That he'd assumed the worst of her? But why?

It was his lack, not hers. His mistrust.

And Emma had not deserved his bitterness any more than Violet had. He was, in fact, unworthy of her love or her devotion.

Swiveling a look at Emma, who was deep in conversation with Elle about something he couldn't make out from here, it was as if he was looking at Violet. Even though he'd told himself that Emma and Violet were not alike at all, he'd been wrong about that, too. Wrong about Violet's faithfulness, her strength to survive when others would have crumpled. Emma, too, had steel beneath the velvet of her soul. She never backed down, despite what had happened to her. That was who she was. Yet she was a modern woman who had options that Violet never had.

If Violet had lived till Emma's age now, Violet's children would have been nearly grown. It gave him small comfort that she'd had her bairns to love amidst the conflict with her husband.

Emma was childless. Unmarried. Alone. Were her chances for a future to be ripped away by feckless destiny just as Violet's had been? Was that to happen to her time after time? What part had he played in her unhappiness? Could releasing her from his own bitterness be the key to freeing her? And himself?

He watched her tip her face up to the sun and close her eyes. This was her world, not his anymore. She wasn't ready to leave it. At thirty-three, she had a long life ahead of her. He'd begun this journey with her, anxious to be done with it, for her to accept her fate and move on. But the longer he was with her, the more he wanted to slow things down. To drag his feet. Stop the inevitable.

The sun poured down on his shoulders. He stared out at the boat Sam Wynter was sailing, wind filling its canvases, pushing it across the lake. He'd watched the love grow for him and Elspeth, watched it change them, redirect their destinies. Forgiveness could heal, of that he had no doubt. But love was a balm to the soul.

He was worthy of neither and felt hardly fit to be a guardian. Yet when he looked at Emma, sitting in the sun beside Elspeth, smiling at something she said, stroking Anika's small head, the urge to wrap his arms around her and pull her against him came swift and strong. As if some band that had been strung tightly around him for so long had come undone. He filled his lungs with the sweet lakeside air, bracing himself. Admitting he'd been wrong was never easy for him. But admitting this...this thing that had held him for so long...

He ran a hand through his hair, lying back against the sun-warmed dock, contemplating how he would navigate those waters.

"Was it bad?" Emma asked, a few minutes later, from somewhere behind him. He jerked upright and shielded his eyes from the sun. She stood over him with a halo of light surrounding her silhouette.

"Aye, it was," he admitted. Elspeth had taken the babe back in the house, and they were alone.

She sat down beside him, dangling her legs over the side of the dock. "I'm...sorry. So, I was wrong, then. About Violet."

"No. Ye were right. I was the one who was wrong."

She said nothing, waiting for his explanation.

"'Twas my fault she ended up with that bastard, Sykes. I could'a saved her that life, but I chose my own anger instead. Chose to duel wi' him. Played right into his hand. If I'd had a square go at him, everything would've been different. But her diary was written to me, ye see. As if she knew someday I'd find it and understand how I'd wronged her."

"Did she say that? That you'd wronged her?"

"No," he admitted. "Didna mean it wasna true."

She smiled at him, brushing his fingers with her own. "I'd point out here that to err is human. But apparently that old platitude is not limited to mortals, since you're still imagining you're actually in control of everything. On the other hand—and I can't believe I'm saying this to an angel— it's possible you've misconceived her intentions."

He scowled at the water, lapping against the wooden dock. "Meaning?"

"Meaning maybe it was her love for you, her abiding love, she wanted you to understand with that diary. Not her blame."

"You're only guessin'." He hated the hopeful note that word struck.

"Maybe, but I feel it here." She fisted a hand against her heart. "I am her, remember? Or so you keep saying. Elspeth reminded me that soul memory is a thing. Maybe that's it. Maybe that's how I know that she loved you and has already forgiven you. Long ago. Far be it for me to advise you, Connor, but I think it's yourself that you need to forgive.

Maybe that's the whole point of this. But what do I know? I'm only human."

He threaded his fingers through hers, that touch affecting him as it always did, sending a current of hunger through him. A jolt of need. She clasped his hand in hers.

"'Tis my stubborn pride kept me from seeing the truth about her," he said, his thumb rubbing across the back of her hand. "Me that's held ye back, put this weight on yer soul, though ye didn't know 'twas me."

"No," she said. "That's not true."

"It is. Marguerite told me. 'Tis a wound that needed binding, or we—you and I—would keep circlin' one another like this, dancin' this dance, until…forever. I never told ye, but we met again once before. During the Great War, it was. You—not Emma, not Violet—were a young nurse named Catherine Belmont, during the Battle of Verdun, in France. I was there for someone else, but I recognized ye then, too. Though ye didn't look like this. But before anything could happen between us, ye died in a shelling. Ye passed young and alone. Again." He felt the shiver of recognition move through her as she tightened her fingers around his.

She stared at him for a long moment. "Whatever you and I have, Connor, however our bond links us, you have to know—my life now is my own. I don't blame anyone else for my choices. Certainly not you or some long ago betrayal. Any road I've taken in this life has been of my own choosing."

"But still," he said. "Yer alone. No bairns. No husband."

She sighed, staring down at the minnows schooling beneath her toes. "This is the twenty-first century, Conner. I am, after all, an independent woman."

"A woman like you isn'a meant to be alone, Emma."

She forced a smile. "Well, you see? Just my luck that the one man who's been in a love/hate relationship with me for centuries, my soul mate, isn't even human. What chance does a girl have?" She dared to look up at him then, and despite her answer, her eyes brimmed with emotion.

"I'm sorry," he murmured, lifting the back of her hand to his lips, kissing her there. "I'm verra sorry, lass."

"No," she said, cupping his jaw with her palm. "You need to put that behind you now, Connor. There's no blame here. Just resolution."

"Then I'm resolved," he whispered, "to imagine what could'a been. For the rest of my days."

She dragged her finger against his lips to stop him from saying more, then, leaning even closer, she kissed him, her lips parting with more than invitation. Demand was what it was. Surprise ceded to need, and he surrendered to her, tugging her closer up against him, until the soft curve of her breasts fit against his chest like a puzzle piece, like they'd been designed to fit together. With her arms around his neck, he lowered her beneath him until they were lying on the sun-warmed wooden dock, his fingers buried in her hair. The ache of mortal need came back to him, crashing over him like a wave.

This woman. So familiar yet so completely not Violet. She belonged—unapologetically—to herself, and he loved that about her. Gone was the anger of that first kiss between them, what once was, rushing away from him with the dizzying speed of the bullet that had taken him down, but in its place, this woman had managed to burrow herself inside him. Now he'd never move past her. Never truly let go of what he felt for her.

With a sound of loss, he broke the kiss and stared down at her, memorizing her face. Her eyes. The forgiveness he found there. The confusion. He pulled her against him. She settled against his chest, and he wrapped his arms around her. It had been a very long time since he'd envied mortals. Since he'd longed for the ups and downs of human consternation and joy, the taste of desire, the burn of need under his skin. Holding her, kissing her reminded him of all that and more. He'd moved into dangerous territory here. This wasn't his purpose in coming. This wasn't about him at all. And he'd broken the one hard-and-fast rule of celestials.

As Elspeth had done before him.

But he was not Elspeth. He would not fall. He had already been appointed to the Council. He had reached his long-sought-after goal. Even if Emma died, there would be none of this there. None of this coming together in mortal pleasure. No children. Just Celestial boundaries. If they saw him now, no doubt it would go against him in his review. It might even disqualify him. But astonishingly, he found he didn't care. Holding her this way felt worth all that after all those centuries of pain.

Let them keep the Council from him. It didn't seem as important now as it once had. He wanted to drag his feet, slow down Emma's path. Whatever it was. But suddenly, he hoped it was not to go with him. She deserved a full life, a mortal man who could share with her all those things she longed for. A home. Family. The chance to grow old together.

Somewhere down the lake, the boom of an early firework exploded over the water, breaking the moment as a cheer and teenaged laughter erupted from the boys whose boat was passing Sam's on the water. Molly waved a miniature flag at them as they gunned their boat across the lake.

"It goes by so fast," Emma murmured, watching the children. "So terribly fast."

He knew she wasn't talking about the boat. "Aye, lass."

"We should get back to the hospital," she said but made no move to untangle herself from him. She tightened her fingers around his, glancing down at the dial on his wrist. Connor looked, too. It read *+85 percent.* She pulled in a long, shaky breath.

"Not yet. Just a little longer," he told her as his palm skimmed her soft hair. "Hey, do ye think they'd mind if we hitched a ride on their boat? Just for a wee bit?"

She sat up with a shocked smile. "You mean—?"

He nodded. "I dinna think Elspeth would rat us out. And they willna know."

Emma tugged him up to his feet with an impish look. An instant later, they were settling themselves on the stern of Sam Wynter's beautiful hand-built sailboat as it cut across the surface of the lake, with the wind in their hair and the July sun caressing their skin.

The fragrance of the clear water, the sky, sharply blue against the green trees—it all reminded him of things he'd forgotten in the shadow of his bitterness, the simple pleasures of the mortal world. Emma soaked up every sunny moment as if it might be her last.

Sam and Molly stood at the wheel a few feet away, not aware of them at all. Sam had his hands atop Molly's as she steered the boat across the open water.

"That's it," he told her. "Now watch the wind, then steer into it. Like this. You want to angle into the waves, not alongside them."

"Can I teach Anika how to sail?" she asked. "When I learn how?"

"You bet. She's a little too small yet. But that's what big sisters are for. By next summer, she and Elspeth will be coming out here every day with us."

"And Iris and Grandpa?" Molly turned directly toward Emma and Connor, then seemed to look right at them. "Mommy would have liked this boat, too, don't you think?" she said.

Taken aback, Emma flicked a look at Connor, who seemed to take Molly's look in stride. "Dinna worry. She canna see us."

"I know your mom would've," Sam told Molly. "And she'd be so proud of her girl."

"Me?"

He tickled her ribs, making her squeal with laughter. "Of course, you! You're her girl, forever and always."

"Maybe she's watching us right now," Molly said. "Maybe she's up there right now, looking at us sailing." Over their heads, a seabird sailed on the air currents, occasionally flapping its wings, mid-glide. Emma's gaze followed it across the lake, remembering what Connor had told her about the child's mother.

"Don't you ever doubt it, Molly-girl," Sam said. "Hey, c'mere. Let me put some more sunscreen on that nose of yours!"

Molly squirmed but finally relented.

Emma watched them for a long time before she leaned against Connor's shoulder. "I'm finding it very ironic to be sitting on this sailboat knowing it's the first time I've done something like this in years. Vacations, for me, were not vacations at all but staff perks. Every 'vacation' I take the company on is spent working, organizing, and worrying that everything will work perfectly. There's very little of…this. Of noticing the way the sun plays across the water or me breathing deeply or even just enjoying watching a child with her father."

Connor, too, appeared to be taken with the pair steering the boat. He smiled a little wistfully. "You're right there, lass."

"And what about you?" she asked. "When was the last time you just purely enjoyed what you were doing? Aside from this?"

Connor scowled thoughtfully. "My work is—"

"No, not your work. What do you do for fun?"

"Fun?" The word rolled off his tongue as if it were foreign.

"Yes, Connor. Something that makes you happy. Makes you laugh or just feel free."

"That isna the point of what I do."

"You mean you're not allowed to—?"

"I'm sayin' 'tis not wholly regarded as critical to our job description."

"But it's not prohibited."

He leaned back against the wooden stern. "And yer point is…?"

"My point is…I'm not sure of my point. Just that if that dial on your wrist is any indication maybe we should enjoy the time we have left. Together."

A muscle worked in his jaw as he thought about her words. "What d'ye suggest?"

"Well," she said, looking up through her lashes at him. "Are those wings of yours practical or only used to impress in-betweeners?"

"What? Ye mean these?" He unfolded his wings effort-lessly, like a proud weightlifter, baring his physique.

She giggled. "Yeah. Those." This time, she touched them, running her fingertips across the soft rows of feathers. "Are they good for anything or…just for show?"

"How is it ye think we get from here to there?"

"I…I couldn't say. It happens so fast."

"In *your* time, it does." His smile hitched something in her chest.

"But wait. I've moved from here to there myself," she said. "And I'm not…how—?"

He cocked his head in agreement. "Nor can ye hold things in your hand. Or show yourself. You're in-between, Emma. Neither quite one o' them right now nor one o' us. But somewhere in the middle. Yer will moves ye, simple as that. Ye think yerself a place, then there ye are."

Ah. "Then," she asked, tucking her hand around his arm, "could we do it your way but slow it down for me? Just once?"

"Slow it down? Ye want to see, is that it?"

"Yes." She took in the beauty of the lake around them, imagining what a bird's-eye view of it might be. Or flying back home, with nothing between them and the earth but air. "I want to see everything. And I want you to see it, too, with me. Maybe it's the last time."

Touched by her words, he tucked his arm around her.

"Then ye shall have it, Emma." He pulled her up beside him. With the rocking of the boat, she collided against him, but he didn't set her away. Instead, he held her for a moment against him, steadied her. Grateful, Emma pressed her cheek to his chest and slid her arms around his waist. His shirt was warmed by the sun. It felt good to be held by him. It felt right.

He pressed a kiss to the top of her head. "Ready?"

Was she? Was she really ready for anything that was about to happen? "No time like the present," she murmured against him, threading her fingers through his. With a swoop of wings and a sound like the wind sifting through the treetops, they were off.

Chapter Nine

K INSEY ABBOTT STOOD outside the ICU holding flowers again as Aubrey returned from a quick trip out for fast food. It was the third time since Emma had been admitted that she'd shown up with flowers. Aubrey approached her with a smile. The closer she got, the more she noticed that her short-cropped hair looked in need of washing. She was still wearing the exact same khakis and long-sleeved shirt she'd been in yesterday and the day before. None of that was normal, but Aubrey decided she must've been under more stress than any of them knew.

"Hey, Kinsey. That's so sweet of you to bring flowers again."

"Emma likes roses. I wanted her to have them."

"I know," Aubrey said, gently. "But listen. I'm sure you didn't know, but they don't allow her to have flowers in the ICU. We've been taking them home until she gets a real room."

"Oh," she replied, not quite meeting Aubrey's eyes.

"But you're right. She'd love them. I'll tell her you brought them. Okay?"

Kinsey held onto the flowers and turned to go.

"You don't want to leave them with me?"

"Maybe I'll come back later," she said without fully turning.

"Hey. How are you doing?" Aubrey asked her.

"Fine." Then she did turn back. If the dark circles under her eyes were any proof, she didn't seem fine. Never very talkative, Kinsey was a bit socially awkward and had never seemed very fond of her. Aubrey didn't know why, since they'd only had a few opportunities to talk in the months Aubrey had worked at Emma's company over the summer.

"I know this has been hard on all of us. I know you've been working overtime keeping things going. Thank you for that."

"Everything's done. I did it for Emma."

"Well, she'd thank you, too, Kinsey, if she could. That will really mean everything to her when she wakes up."

"Will she?"

"Will she...what?"

"Wake up? I asked the nurses, but they wouldn't tell me anything."

She gestured Kinsey over to a waiting room chair, which she reluctantly took. Aubrey sat down beside her. "They're hopeful. That's what I know. They pulled back on the meds that were keeping her in a coma after her surgery. She's off intubation. They're trying to wake her. Now it's just time. Her leg is healing. If her body is healing, then her brain will, too."

Kinsey picked off a petal from a rose, rolling it between her fingers. "It shouldn't have happened."

"Yeah. No, it shouldn't have. We'll find the person who did it. They'll pay, believe me. Regardless, she'll have a long recovery. But Emma's unstoppable. Everyone knows that."

"If she dies, then it'll all go to you. Won't it?"

Taken aback, Aubrey blinked at her. "I know you didn't mean that to sound the way it came out, Kinsey, because Emma's going to live."

Kinsey blushed, but Aubrey's hackles were up. Emma's assistant's "edit" button was quite different from other people's. While everyone gave her space for that little idiosyncrasy, right now, Aubrey's nerves were stretched thin.

"I'm sorry." Kinsey dropped the bouquet to her side. "I didn't mean it."

Aubrey stood. "Okay. This is stressful on all of us. I'm going to go in to see her now. Take care, Kinsey. Get some rest. Do you want me to take the flowers to Emma's home?"

Kinsey frowned and, without reply, stood and hurried away down the hall.

Aubrey couldn't help feeling upset. Edit buttons aside, there was something about Kinsey that had always rubbed her the wrong way. Emma had hired her eight years ago, and she pretty much handled the contracts department like a pro. Numbers, details were her thing. People were not. Obviously. Aubrey recalled Emma mentioning that Kinsey had asked her about joining the firm as an associate agent. They both knew the problems with that. Now with that comment, Aubrey wondered if Kinsey was somehow jealous of her relationship with Emma.

Would I inherit the company? What kind of question was that? She was twenty-three with no experience in real estate except what she'd done this summer alongside Emma. No one, least of all her, would imagine she could run the firm the way Emma did. Or that even Emma would imagine she could. But all of that speculation was neither here nor there. Emma was going to live. That's all there was to it.

At the nurses' station, she stopped to talk to Mary, the charge nurse. "Any change?"

Mary sent her a sympathetic look. "Not really. I'm sorry."

"Have you spoken with the doctor?"

"She should be here in the next few minutes. You can speak to her then."

Aubrey went into Emma's room and sat down beside her. It had been a long three days, and the optimism she was showing the world about Emma's condition was not exactly what she felt deep inside. Scared was what she felt. Alone. Foolishly, she'd thought Emma would wake twenty-four hours after the accident, then they could move on, putting this whole awful thing behind them. But that hadn't happened. The longer her coma lasted, the smaller the odds she would awaken at all. A second brain scan this morning showed that her brain was still working, active even, but she couldn't seem to wake up.

Aubrey took her hand. "Emma. Can you hear me? I need you to come back now. Wake up."

She got no response from Emma. Not even a little squeeze of her fingers. "Did you know tomorrow's the Fourth of July? You never miss the Fourth. The park is all decked out. The fireworks are ready to go. There'll be a parade of bicycles. All the kids will decorate their own at the booth you started a few years ago. Crepe paper. Flags. Playing cards on their spokes. And the donuts, Em. Everyone loves them. They were your idea, too. Everyone's asked about you. Everyone misses you. So, you really have no choice here. Can you hear me?"

Doctor Callonet stepped through the sliding glass door with Emma's chart in her hands. She reached for Aubrey's. "Hi, Aubrey. How's she doing?"

"I was going to ask you that question. How is she?"

The doctor glanced at her charts for a moment. "The good news—her vitals are all good. She's breathing well. Her oxygen is good. Her levels are all pretty much where we'd want to see them. She made it through the surgery with flying colors. We had hoped she'd be waking by now, but she's still in a coma. We're not sure why."

"And if she doesn't wake soon?"

She hung the chart at the end of the bed. "We'll be moving her out of the ICU tonight and bringing her to a regular room. After that, she'll be heading to a rehab facility."

"A rehab facility? But if she's not awake, how can she rehab?"

"Let's not go there yet. It's only been a few hours since we lifted the sedation. Let's see what happens."

Aubrey nodded because the alternative wasn't something she could even contemplate right now.

"Your aunt has a lot going for her. She's young, fit, and a fighter. You need to try to stay positive for the both of you."

"Doctor, tell me the truth. You've seen patients go through things like this before. Do you think she'll be okay?"

Dr. Callonet sent Aubrey a gentle smile. "I try to never second-guess the powers that be. But I always try to err on the side of hope."

When she'd gone, Aubrey sat beside Emma again and pressed her forehead to the back of her aunt's hand. "I'm right here. Can you feel me? Please. Hurry back."

PERHAPS THIS WAS *all just a dream,* Emma thought as they arrived back at the hospital parking lot after a heart-thumping, breath-stealing ride back with Connor. All of this was beyond her imagining. The longer she was separated from the world she'd known, the less she found herself bound to it. For heaven's sake, she'd just flown halfway down the coast with an angel! Perhaps this was the way it happened. The going. Little by little until the loss wasn't so shocking or too great. Until the alternative seemed not so terrifying.

Maybe he'd agreed to humor her because he knew she was almost there. Or because she'd realized, somehow, that Aubrey would survive without her. Her niece had her own angels he'd told her, and she guessed that much was true. If nothing else, this time with Connor had taught her that she was truly in control of nothing but her own happiness, despite imagining the opposite for most of her life. It was exhausting, trying to control everything. She'd never realized just how exhausting it was. How futile.

She felt so far away from the woman lying in that bed upstairs. So disconnected. But every moment that passed with Connor brought her closer and closer to some indefinable end she knew she wasn't prepared for. Whether she lived or whether she died, whether she woke or not, this man beside her would disappear from her life. And it made her heart ache.

How ridiculous. How perfectly ironic that at Death's door, she'd found herself falling in love with her guardian angel—a soul mate she could never have.

After I'm finished here, he'd said to Elspeth not an hour ago about ascending to the Council, whatever that was. After he'd finished with her was what he'd meant. Finished resolving wherever she was heading. And then, they would be over.

As if they were a "they" at all. Yes, he'd kissed her on the dock and, of course, there had been that angry kiss in the hospital. But all of that, she realized, was just his process of letting her—and Violet—go. He'd said as much when he'd first met her.

And now, with his hand in hers, they walked through the parking lot—a metaphor, of sorts, for her life—still not knowing what lay ahead. Which was, she supposed, for the best. Because she wasn't sure anymore what the right decision for herself was.

Ahead, she saw Jacob—Aubrey's Jacob—exiting his car. She wanted to run to him, to throw her arms around him. Thank him for being there for Aubrey. She'd underestimated him. He was good for Aubrey, and she had chosen well. She wanted to tell him all of those things, but, of course, she couldn't.

She checked her emotions, rising at the thought that she might never get the chance. She shouldn't have been afraid to go. Not now. Now that she knew what her gran had known all along. That angels existed and she'd never be truly alone.

Connor squeezed her hand as another car pulled up near Jacob, and Aaron Pleasure got out. The midday sun cast long shadows around them.

"Hey, you're Emma's friend, aren't you?" Jacob asked, reaching a hand out to him.

Aaron smiled. "I am. Aaron Pleasure. And you're…?"

"Jacob. I'm Aubrey's...boyfriend—for lack of a better term. I saw you here the other day, didn't I? To see Emma?"

"Yeah. I was just coming back to check on her. They won't tell me anything on the phone. How's she doing?"

Jacob rubbed a hand across his mouth. "No change yet. Unfortunately. They took her off the heavy meds, but so far, she's not waking up. They don't really know why."

Maybe I'm not ready to. Maybe I don't know how any of this works. Emma flicked a look at Connor, who was watching the two men intensely.

"I'm sorry to hear that," Aaron said, shaking his head. She noticed a little gray at his temples and a few more lines on his face than he'd had the last time they'd been together. But he still had that boyish charm about him she'd always loved.

"I was hoping when I came into town I would get to see her, you know? Actually, I was hoping we could have a cup of coffee. I don't know. See what happens? Our lives just went two different directions, but she's always been in the back of my mind. Stupid. I guess you always think there's time."

Connor raised an *I told you so* brow at Emma. She had to agree with Aaron about that much.

Jacob nodded. "Timing. I'm sorry it worked out that way. But keep the faith. We're not giving up. You shouldn't, either. I know Aubrey said Emma talked about you often. Anything's possible."

Connor let loose of her hand just as another figure hurried out of the hospital doors. It took Emma a minute to recognize her. It was Kinsey. She seemed...upset—something in the way she marched across the parking lot.

The two men also noticed her, too. They turned to watch as she reached her SUV parked ten or more cars down from them and furiously beat the front fender with the bouquet in her hand. She hit the car until there was nothing but stumps left of the flowers before finally climbing in and gunning it out of the parking lot.

"Whoa," Aaron said.

Jacob blinked in shock. "What the hell? That was Kinsey."

"Who?"

"She works for Emma. Wonder what got her all bent?"

"'Bent' is one word for it," Aaron said.

Their gazes both followed Kinsey's car as it pulled out onto the main road, squealing its tires.

"Hey, I don't want to play devil's advocate here," Aaron said, "but didn't Aubrey say that the car that hit Emma was a dark SUV?"

Jacob swiveled a look at him. "Yeah?"

"Did you happen to notice that front fender she was whacking with the flowers?"

"No. I was just kind of waiting for her to morph into the Hulk or something. But now that you mention it, it was banged up. You don't think..."

"I don't know what to think after that."

"Yeah. Well. I think it's worth looking into," Jacob said, pulling his phone from his back pocket. "And worth a phone call to the detective."

Emma stared after Kinsey's car, too, cold trickling through her. Kinsey? No, it couldn't have been her. She would never—And what about Emma's house getting trashed? Looking like someone had…rage-stormed through it?

Rage-stormed.

Kinsey demolishing those flowers came to mind.

And then she remembered—Kinsey had a key to her house. Of course she did. Emma had given it to her once years ago so she could feed Winston while Emma had been traveling to visit Aubrey at college. Kinsey had done that for her several times over the years. And one time, she remembered returning from her bedroom retrieving papers only to find Kinsey staring at the photos on her shelf of her and Aubrey. Of Lizzy and Daniel. Of the loving family Kinsey had never really had.

A thousand jagged emotions swam through her. Disbelief, first. Anger. Followed quickly by the love she'd always had for Kinsey. For everything Kinsey had done for her company, for her personally.

Beside her, Connor, too, watched her car disappear down the road. He watched Jacob and Aaron head into the hospital.

"We need to follow her," Emma said. "I'm…afraid for her."

He gave her a sideways look. "Aye. So am I. But I didna expect that to be yer lead feelin' here."

"Am I angry? Yes," she said, tugging him along beside her toward the road. "But I must have missed something. Something important."

"Ye think it's all your fault she ran ye off the road?"

"I…I think it's my fault I wasn't paying attention to what she must have been going through. Connor. Please. Let's follow her."

He nodded. "I ken where she's goin'."

They arrived at Kinsey's car parked on the road that ran along the Schooner's Bay cliffs, which led to a trail above them. Together, they walked the trail that Emma had walked so many times before, a perilous trail with cliffs on one side and a rocky drop on the other. This part of the trail led to a safer scenic outlook that most kids in Schooner's Bay eventually took full advantage of as a make-out place after dark. But it had its perils. Like now.

Kinsey stood on the side of the cliff, staring at the rocks below and at the ocean of blue that stretched out before her. There were tears in her eyes as she paced across the edge of the cliff, furiously puffing on a cigarette. Emma saw how she might have been mistaken for a man that night in the dark with her short-cropped hair and boyish look.

Emma's heart clenched. This was what she'd feared. Kin-

CALLING ALL ANGELS

sey had always presented a tough exterior to the world, but she knew that inside she was fragile as a sparrow. She should have been more careful with her words, with her friendship. "Kinsey, *don't!*"

"She canna hear ye."

"I know." But how long had that been going on in real life? Kinsey, being unable to hear her? Or grasp how she'd felt about her? Too long. "You need to talk to her for me. Tell her what I say. Word for word."

"Ye want me to let her see me?"

"Yes, Connor! Yes."

"Even if I do, she willna remember me later. Or even what I say."

"Then I'll tell her. If I can. We'll worry about that then. For now just, please, do as I ask. Do it for me, Connor? This one thing."

Reluctantly, he nodded, walking gingerly toward Kinsey on the cliff.

Hearing his footsteps behind her, Kinsey whirled back in Connor's direction, and he threw his hands up before him to indicate that he meant her no harm.

"It's Kinsey, isn't it?" he asked in a quiet voice.

"Who are you?" she demanded. "Go away!"

"I'm not here to hurt ye, lass. I'm here to help ye."

"I don't want your help," she said, stepping closer to the cliff's edge. "Leave me alone!"

"I'm here for Emma," he told her.

187

"What?" Kinsey blinked at him, confused.

"Emma James. I know ye'll find this hard to believe, but she wants me to tell ye somethin'."

"Emma James is dying. She can't tell me anything." She tossed what was left of her cigarette over the cliff.

"Oh, but yer wrong there. She's right here, watchin' ye. She wants to speak to ye."

"You're…you're crazy," Kinsey said, her eyes going wide. "Stay away from me! Get back!"

"All right, then. I understand why you'd think that, but—"

"Tell her you're an angel," Emma said beside him. "Tell her you're *my* angel."

"*Och*, that should seal the deal," he muttered, unconvinced.

"It can't get any worse," she pointed out. "Tell her. Word for word."

Kinsey was staring at him now, seemingly uncertain which option posed her the most danger, this stranger talking to himself or the rocks below.

"Ye see," he began slowly, holding his flattened palm out to Kinsey, "I'm not exactly…what ye think. I'm no threat to ye, Kinsey. I'm Emma's guardian. Her guardian angel."

Kinsey's eyes widened in fear. "Her…what?"

"I know how it sounds. But 'tis true. Believe it or don't, but she wants ye to know somethin'."

"Okay. I really am losing my mind," Kinsey breathed as

soil crumbled beneath the toe of her shoe. "I was right. I'm crazy."

"No… No," he said, repeating the words Emma spoke. "You're not. Listen to me. Emma says she knows you didn't mean to hurt her."

"Emma says…*what?*"

"She knows that you care about her. That ye didn't mean it. The car…"

Kinsey shook her head, tears burning in her eyes, searching the empty space beside him for signs of Emma. "How did you—? How can you know about—?"

"I'm speakin' for her, ye see? She knows it was you."

Kinsey's expression crumbled. "I didn't. I didn't mean it. It was all a mistake." A sob broke her words. "A h-horrible mistake."

"She knows that," he told her. "She knows you'd never mean to hurt her—or Aubrey, either."

Kinsey lowered her head. "I did, though. I did hurt her. I was s-so mad about everything. At Emma not believing in me. Aubrey just walking into every opening so easy. Aubrey has everything…I have no one. I just…I don't know what happened. I just lost control." She pressed her fingertips to her skull. "Why am I telling you this? There's no changing things. I did what I did."

"What's done is done, you're right. But, Kinsey, 'tis wrong to think Emma didna care about you. She did. She does." He glanced at Emma, who motioned for him to go

189

on. "She's sorry for not payin' better attention to what you wanted. She knows it's hard for you to accept help. But things can get better. And they will if you'll try."

"It's too late for me. I even went to her house to tell Aubrey what I did, to apologize, but she was already gone, and then…I couldn't help it. I messed up her house because I'd ruined everything. Now Emma's…she must be *dead* because if you're an angel—? It's all my fault."

"She's not dead. And the part of her that loves ye is right here beside me. But this here…this is no answer."

Beside him, Emma nodded, encouraging him as Kinsey inched toward the edge.

"She says she forgives ye, Kinsey, for what happened. She wants to help ye."

For the first time, there was a shred of hope in Kinsey's eyes. "No, she doesn't."

"Aye. She does. She said so herself. Right here."

"I don't believe you."

Connor tipped his head as Emma instructed him what to say. "She asks if ye remember the time it was just the two of you workin' late and she ordered a pizza with pineapple and Canadian bacon—your favorite—and ye told her about your third foster mom. How she'd read ye stories at night? How she was the only one who ever did that for ye?"

Kinsey gaped at him.

"How she'd read ye the story of King Arthur pulling that sword from the stone, and how ye said that someday you'd do that? That she told ye—"

"I could be anything I wanted to be," Kinsey finished. "How could you possibly know that?"

"I told you. Emma's right here wi' me. If ye have somethin' to say to her, say it now. Go on, lass."

She swallowed thickly, tears running down her cheeks. "This is crazytime. But…I'm…I'm sorry, Emma. If you can hear me, I'm so sorry. I wish I could take that night back. I'd give anything if I could."

Connor held his hand out to her as a siren sounded in the distance. "Take my hand, lass. Come away from here. You'll sort it out. It'll be all right, ye hear?"

Kinsey glanced one more time at the rocks below, then reached for his hand just as the sandy ground beneath her foot began to crumble.

With a wide-eyed look of terror, Kinsey gasped, but Connor snagged her arm and caught her, pulling her almost effortlessly back up beside him. With a sob of gratitude, she crumped to the ground, shaking. The simple act of trust sent a rush of relief through Emma. It gave her hope that Kinsey would get through this somehow. That she'd come out the other side.

Connor disappeared from sight as two uniformed police officers—a man and a woman—appeared around the bend in the trail.

Kinsey saw them, too, but made no move to run. She glanced behind her to find Connor gone. A look of disbelief crossed her expression.

"Kinsey Abbott?" the woman called, approaching her gently with her hand out. Reluctantly, Kinsey nodded. "We'd like a word with you."

Chapter Ten

THE NEXT DAY, as Aubrey clicked off on her cell-phone call with the detective, she leaned her head against Jacob's shoulder outside the private room Emma had been moved to. Still shaken with disbelief that it could have been Kinsey all along, she wrapped her arm around Jacob's waist as Aaron leaned against the wall nearby beneath a Fourth of July banner and photos of the staff's celebrations from years past. Little red, white, and blue flags were strung across the nurse's station. The nurses were already passing out slices of a patriotic flag cake someone had baked.

All that seemed surreal against the backdrop of what they'd learned.

"How did we not see it?" she asked. "That she was so angry or…or jealous of my relationship with Emma?"

"She never showed you any of that?" Aaron asked.

"No. Not really. We weren't really friends, but she must have been holding in all those feelings. When they finally came out, it was a big, awful mess. Jacob, we were right about the mix-up. She apparently thought it was me in that car, driving. It was me she was angry with." Jacob wrapped his arm around her shoulder. "And the house? That was just pure out-of-control Kinsey, understanding that she had royally messed everything up. Poor Emma paid the price."

"At least now we don't have to keep looking over our shoulders," Jacob said. "Thanks to you, Aaron, for putting it together about her car."

Aaron folded his arms across his chest. "Dumb luck, I guess. They're arresting her, right?"

Aubrey nodded. "She admitted to everything. But because she was up on that cliff, possibly to harm herself, they've put a thirty-six-hour psych hold on her at a hospital over in Portland. Also," she added, "possibly because she first claimed she was talking to an angel out there on the cliff. Who also claimed to be talking to Emma." Aubrey shook her head. "Can you believe that? As if it weren't bad enough, she almost killed Emma, but she has to drag her into her fantasy confession. Later, she acted like she had no idea what they were talking about when they brought it up."

"It's going to break Emma's heart to learn it was her," Jacob said.

The worry written on Aubrey's face said it all. "I hope," she whispered against his shoulder, "I hope she gets the chance to learn what really happened. Then at least we'll have Emma back."

CONNOR AND EMMA, who had been listening silently, left them then and moved into her new private room. This room was much better than the ICU had been, with a big window spanning one wall, where the spectacle of the sunset over the Pacific would be a nightly ritual, and a cozy chair and lamp sat in one corner for guests. Her color looked better. She looked, Connor thought, like she was sleeping. But waking she was not.

Emma stood over the bed, staring at her body. She wasn't urging herself to wake up. Nor hoping she wouldn't wake. She was caught between those two things, with him, squarely in the middle.

He understood the emotions churning through her. With everything that had come at her in the last few days she was dizzy with feelings even he couldn't decipher. Feelings that included a messy, conflicted sadness regarding him. That was all his fault.

She moved past him to stand at the window, looking out at the green summer trees and the hills surrounding the hospital. She wanted out, he sensed. Out of here. Away from the possibility of dying. She wanted to be flying again. Looking down from above without worry.

"Do you think," she asked him, "I'll be stuck here forever? In this in-between place?"

He moved beside her at the window. "I dinna think so, lass."

"What makes you so sure?"

"There's a finite end to this. One way or the other. At least Marguerite promised me so."

"Right. The Council for you. But what about me? What if," she began gingerly, "what if I'm damaged and I can't— What if I said that I wanted to stay with you? To go. Not stay here."

Now it was his turn to stare out the window without really seeing. "Even if ye could choose for yerself, Emma, that's no' how this works."

"Then how *does* it work?"

He swallowed hard. "If goin' was your path, I'm afraid I've got a few hundred years on ye in experience. Our paths would diverge. You and I...well, we wouldn't be possible."

"You're saying I can't choose?"

"Most would stay if the choice was theirs, no? But every life has a season. Whether it's summer or winter, autumn or spring that draws that life to a close, it's the right time to start again. The absolute right time. And it's without regret. Because now they know, behind them, the angels are watchin' over those they loved, helpin' them find their own way."

"My gran believed that," she said. "But...I still miss her."

"I know. Emma," he began, "my hope is if ye stay, you'll forget me and this time together. It's just as well if ye do."

"And if I go?"

"Then you'll move on. Free from me as well."

She stared out at the changing sky. "I see. So, tell me the

truth, then. Why did you kiss me back there on the dock? Was it just…to let me go?"

"Ye don't really think that, do ye?"

Emma leaned against the window ledge. "What should I think?"

He glanced at his wrist: +94 percent. "That our time is almost up and whatever ye needed to push ye forward here is nearly done." But that felt like a half-truth because he sensed some season had passed in him as well, though he couldn't say what that meant. "I kissed ye for selfish reasons—none of which were about lettin' ye go, I'm sorry to say. If ye asked my superiors about my behavior, then you'd likely to get an earful from them. And worse. But I don't care. What I know is you're free to move forward now, without my bitterness— or accusation—draggin' ye down in whatever ye choose for yerself. That's the best I could do for ye here."

Disappointment filtered through her expression as she glanced out the window at the sky, turning a deepening shade of blue and pink and red. "Look. It's nearly sunset. They'll be setting off the fireworks at the park. I say we go before that clock on your wrist strikes midnight and our coach turns back into a pumpkin."

"Coach?"

"Never mind," she said with a smile, taking his hand. "Just take me to the park, kind sir. It's stifling in here, and I need the air."

He tried to memorize the feel of her fingers against his,

the dark color of her eyes, and the way she smiled up at him just now. He would need that memory for later, when he wanted to replay this moment in his mind. Council or no Council, rules or no, he would not easily rid himself of the memory of these last few days. No matter what white lies of kindness he told her.

"As ye wish, *mo ghràdh*. As ye wish."

THE USUAL FOURTH of July buzz resonated in the evening air at the Schooner's Bay Community Park, where hundreds of people had been celebrating already for hours. Savory-smelling smoke from smoldering barbecues drifted on the air along with the sulfur tang of dozens of sparklers being waved around in the dark by children, whose decorated bikes were scattered around the field, abandoned for now.

The twenty-piece orchestra stationed in the central gaze-bo was playing familiar Fourth of July fare, and around the grassy park, children chased one another in games of tag and keep-away. Parents, drinking wine and hot chocolate from flasks and thermoses, gathered with neighbors and friends to listen to the music.

Emma felt the tension in her shoulders release a fraction at the sight. This felt…normal. A night she would have taken for granted only a few days ago. But now she saw all of it differently, as a moment to be savored. Remembered. The easy comradery of friends making time for one another, stopping to enjoy the moment. Smell the fireworks, so to speak.

She pressed four fingers against her mouth. She'd come to this place year after year, and yes, she'd enjoyed the show, but it hadn't struck her until now how important the friendships that were built on moments like this were. How much time they deserved. How much appreciation.

But even more than that, being separated from all of them made her realize how much she missed them. How much she would miss them if things went the wrong way for her.

And yet the world went on spinning without her in it. Those friends' lives continued while she watched from afar. As it should be, she supposed.

It reminded her of the first time she'd gone to Paris, the city of lights, whose history was as ancient as it was rich. There she'd stood, in the Place de la Concorde between the bronze fountain full of gods and an Egyptian obelisk, in a street full of Parisians, all going about their lives as they did every day, while she, on the other side of the world, had until that moment been completely unaware of their lives or their struggles. And they of hers. She didn't matter a bit in the greater scheme of things. She'd felt so small and insignificant then, but also like a single, solitary cog in the great wheel that was this planet.

That feeling surged again in her now. Emma the outsider. Emma the insignificant. Yet now she saw she was part of something much greater than she could have imagined.

As they walked among the spread-out blankets, deftly avoiding small children and leashed dogs who often noticed them walking past, Mayor Marks took the microphone at the gazebo. "Who's ready for some spectacular fireworks? Anyone? Anyone?"

The crowd roared with applause, and he quieted them finally with a gesture. "But first, can we please say thank you to this amazing orchestra? Aren't they incredible folks?"

Again, the crowd showed their appreciation.

"This has been a wonderful day here at the park," the mayor continued. "But before we get to the fireworks, I just want to say a word here. So many people help this event to happen, not the least of which are all the volunteers that helped us decorate and set up chairs. All the extra food and treats. But honestly, we have one true friend of this celebration, who, every year, donates time and money to make it happen, fundraising with some of her friends in the business community here in Schooner's Bay. Without fail, she is here every year, too, to help us celebrate. But this year, she's in the hospital. She's needing our prayers. So, I'd like to ask for a moment of silence for Emma James. Please keep her in your thoughts tonight as you watch the show, and we wish her a speedy recovery from the accident that put her in the hospital this Fourth of July. Thanks, everyone, and enjoy the show."

The shock of the mayor's words reverberated through Emma. Really? For her? She couldn't believe it as the whole audience fell silent. That silence lasted almost thirty seconds before the first firework exploded overheard, bursting into a brilliant ball of red, white, and blue.

Connor's fingers tightened around hers. "Did ye think they'd forget about ye?"

Emma shook her head. "I never imagined they'd even noticed I'm gone."

"Perhaps ye underestimate your impact here. You're not gone yet. C'mon." He tugged her with him toward the small office building at the edge of the park, where they settled on the low-slung roof. "'Tis the best view from here."

Overhead, the sky had darkened to a velvety black, and a wash of stars lit the backdrop as the fireworks exploded above them.

"You've done this before?" she asked. "Sit here on the rooftops, watching?"

"Oh, aye. Ye'd be hard pressed to find a guardian who wouldn't take a moment to sit in the murk an' watch this."

"Drawn to the sparkles, are you?"

He grinned. "Perhaps. Or it could be the whistlin'. Or just the plain spectacle of it all."

If she ever got out of this, she'd never attend another fireworks show without looking for interloping angels on every rooftop.

They sat for a while in companionable silence, watching

the show, leaning against one another. Emma curled her fingers around his arm. His lips brushed the top of her head and rested there for a moment as he inhaled her scent. "Ye dinna tell me if Elspeth was able to tell ye about yer sister, Lizzy, and her husband."

A double heart-shaped firework exploded above their heads. "She did," Emma said. "She told me she remembered them. It was not what we thought."

"Her memory about her file work is almost photographic. What did she tell you?"

"We all assumed someone had boarded their boat— pirates, maybe, or someone who knew what they were hunting for. Maybe they set them out to sea or murdered them outright, we guessed. But Elspeth says a storm was to blame. Lizzy was blown off the deck and her tether broke. Daniel went in after her. But the sea was impossible and she'd blown too far for him to reach her with his tether, so he unhooked himself. He would have done that. I can't imagine him doing anything else to be honest. So, they died together. They left this Earth together. If there's any comfort here, it's knowing they died doing what they loved."

"At least ye know now."

She nodded. "Elspeth is very kind. I liked her. I think we would be friends if…" She looked up at him as a singer with the orchestra in the gazebo struck up a song from Katy Perry about fireworks as the show cranked up the volume. She rested her head back on Connor's shoulder. "Can I ask you something personal?"

"Depends."

"On whether you trust me enough to answer?"

"I trust ye," he said, surprising her raising her knuckles to his lips, pressing a kiss there. "But tell me the question."

"Was Elspeth happy as a Celestial?" She hesitated. "Are you?"

Connor looked up at the sky, as if he could somehow find an answer there. "*Happiness* is a relative word, isn't it? I canna compare mine to hers. Nor yours to mine. 'Tis subjective, aye?"

"That, Farm Boy, is a nonanswer."

"Fair enough." He braced one wrist on his bent knee. "'Tis a word I ken I havna thought about for a verra long time. Content, I'd say. Mostly. Though if you ask Marguerite, she'd probably say otherwise." His fingers tightened around hers. "I canna do this there." He leaned closer. "Or this." Inhaling the scent of her, his mouth traced the outline of her cheek without quite touching. "Or, especially, this." He took her mouth with his and slid his hand through her hair, pulling her closer.

He tasted of the sweet night air and some indefinable flavor that belonged to him alone. Maybe it was the flavor of an angel. Maybe all angels tasted this good. She doubted it. But most of all, she didn't want him to stop.

Explosions burst above their heads. Fans of color and icicles of white fell from the sky, then burst a second time into balls and flags of red and blue. In the distance, the crowd oohed and aahed over the show. Emma almost forgot where she was as he deepened the kiss, stealing away every bit of her self-control just before she felt the nudge of a cold nose against her arm and the appearance of a dog beside her, wagging his tail.

Connor broke the kiss at the sight of him, but the dog settled his curly little self against her knees, untroubled by the fireworks going off overhead or the fact that Connor had been kissing her.

"*Enoch?*" Connor said, sounding exasperated.

Emma reached out tentatively and scratched the pup behind his ears. "How did you get up here?"

But Connor was not looking at the dog. Instead, his focus was on the woman who had settled herself on the rooftop nearby them. "Marguerite?"

Marguerite? Had Connor somehow conjured her up by speaking her name a few moments ago?

"What a night for a fireworks show, no?" she responded, smiling slyly at Connor. "*Bonjour, ma fille.* Emma, is it not?"

She nodded warily. Emma glanced past the woman to notice others now, sitting on the roof, faces turned up to the sky. More were perched in branches of nearby trees and sitting by twos atop telephone poles. All—

"Guardians," Marguerite confirmed. "*Mais oui.* You see? There's Henry. I think you 'ave met." She pointed to a play structure Henry was standing atop beside several others.

Henry nodded to her but pulled his attention immediately back to the exploding lights in the sky. The more she looked, the more she spotted—angels seemingly drawn here to the spectacle like moths to a flame.

Connor tightened his fingers around Emma's. "There must be a thousand fireworks shows tonight. What can we do for ye here?"

His tone suggested there was nothing she could want that he could give her, but she smiled at him nonetheless. "We?" she repeated. "*Non, mon ami.* Not you both. You have done all you can do—and a good job of it, too. I'm afraid, though, it is time for Emma to go."

Emma inhaled sharply, turning to Connor, wide-eyed with fear. She wasn't ready. She hadn't prepared herself. Adrenaline rocketed through her like the explosion of lights above them.

He tugged her closer to him. "*No.* Not yet. She's no' ready."

"But then, who is, eh?" Marguerite asked, her gaze on Emma.

Enoch licked her hand comfortingly, and Emma knew with absolute certainty that dogs were true angels on Earth. She blinked back the sudden tears that filled her eyes. "Connor? I—I'm afraid."

Emma watched him glance down at the dial on his wrist: +94 percent! He held it out to show Marguerite as if to prove that his task with her was incomplete.

"This is wrong. See? I'm askin' ye, Marguerite."

The older woman tilted a sympathetic look at him. "Ah, Boo. I'm surprised you haven't yet realized. That dial on your wrist…it was never about her, *mon ami*. It was about you."

In shock, Connor stared at the dial as if he'd never seen it before.

"You must come now. It's time." Marguerite held out her hand to Emma.

Inexplicably compelled, Emma obliged, and Marguerite's fingers closed around hers. They felt so different from his but still comforting somehow. The woman pulled Emma to her feet. The dog leapt up, too, wagging his way over to stand beside Connor.

"But…wait!" she stammered. "I—I'm not ready!"

Beside her, Connor's jaw worked. She could see him fighting what he wanted to say. Instead, his eyes met hers with a kind of desperation. Desperation and surrender.

"But you are," Marguerite argued. "You're more than ready now."

"'Twill be all right, *mo ghràdh*," Connor told Emma, his mouth still bruised by her kiss. "She's right. Ye must go. Ye'll be all right now." But he wore an expression she'd never seen on him before, and it scared her. Where was she going?

Marguerite pulled her away from him, and Emma felt herself falling, fading. The park, the fireworks, the sound from the orchestra, all of them disappearing behind her.

Worst of all—

"Connor!" she called out as the space between them widened and the fireworks crescendo overhead exploded in a final overpowering finale. "Don't leave me! Please! Wait! Will I ever see you again?"

But he was on his feet, the July evening breeze tugging at his too-long hair, but he didn't reply. He only stared after her as the sky, the angels on the rooftops, and the crowds in the park grew farther and farther away.

And then, Conner, along with all the rest, disappeared behind her.

Chapter Eleven

E MMA OPENED HER eyes with a gasp. She blinked as the too-bright room she found herself in swam into a blurry focus beyond her lashes.

There was white. Lots of white. A bright light coming from somewhere to her...left? She sensed people. Several people nearby. But moving her head seemed like an over-whelming task, so she slid her gaze sideways and saw—

"She's awake!" Aubrey practically shouted. "Look! Some-one call a doctor! She's awake! *Emma!* Emma, can you hear me? Oh, thank God!"

She felt Aubrey's hand holding hers—but she wanted Connor's hand instead. She opened her mouth to speak, but only a croak came out.

Aubrey leaned closer. "What? What is it, Em? You're okay. You're right here with me. Jacob's here, too. You had an accident. Do you remember?"

But Emma wanted to close her eyes. Return to where she had just been. Because she couldn't see Connor anywhere in the room. And she needed to see him.

Some machine beeped beside her on its tall table, echoing her erratic heartbeat. Now Jacob leaned over the bed, too. "You're getting her too excited. You're okay, Emma."

She shook her head no. She was not okay. She was not going to be okay. "Did you," she croaked very slowly, "see him?"

Aubrey sent a confused look at Jacob. "See who?"

Emma tried to say his name but couldn't get the word out without choking up.

"What did she say?"

"I couldn't make it out," Aubrey said. "Oh no. We've made her cry. It's okay, honey. Don't cry."

"She's bound to be a little confused," Jacob whispered. "Don't press her now."

They were talking about her as if she wasn't in the room. But she knew they hadn't seen him or Marguerite, either. Both of them were gone. From the sunlight pouring through the window, time had clearly passed as well. Who even knew what day this was?

But Aubrey was here. Jacob. Just seeing them still here for her—as they'd been through her whole ordeal—meant everything.

"No," she whispered emphatically, taking Aubrey's hand in hers. "Love you, Aub. Thank...you."

Tears erupted from Aubrey, too, and she leaned down to hug her fiercely. "I love you, too, Em. I'm so glad you're back."

Emma suddenly became aware of something in her left

209

hand. She tightened her fist around it, exploring the warm metal shape. Instantly, she knew what it was and, of course, how it had gotten there.

Jacob saw it, too, and inhaled sharply. "What the—?"

Slowly, she turned her fist up for Aubrey to see.

Aubrey frowned as Emma opened her fingers. Lizzy's peace-symbol necklace spilled out onto the white sheets. "Oh. My—"

"Is that—?" Jacob stammered to a stop.

They stared at it, disbelievingly for a long, long beat.

"How in the world—?"

"No freaking way," he finished.

Aubrey lifted up the necklace by two fingers. The precious green stone in the middle sparkled in the sunlight pouring in the window.

Emma whispered, "Lizzy sends…her…love."

Nine months later…

AUBREY POURED TWO glasses of very nice Chardonnay and slid one across the marble island countertop to Emma. "Honestly, Emma," she said, "a visit to a shrink would be way cheaper than a random trip to Scotland."

Emma tapped her glass against Aubrey's. First, that likely wasn't altogether accurate, and second, there would be no talking her out of this. She had her ticket and her suitcase packed. "I don't need a shrink, and I've made up my mind. I'm going."

"This obsession you have with Scotland is—"

"Weird. Go on. Say it."

"I'm just worried about you, Em. You're just getting back on track at work again. And your leg... I'm worried about you going all alone. What if you fall? What if—"

"I'm going to be fine. You have to stop worrying about me." With five months of occupational therapy, and another few for the rehab for her leg behind her now, she'd put away the cane she'd used throughout the last nine months. She finally felt strong again. Herself again.

Almost.

"If you're just dying for a trip," Aubrey went on, "there are closer places to take a vacation and far nicer weather than freezing cold Scotland in the spring. We could go to the beach. Florida, for instance. I've seen some great rentals down at a place called Rosemary Beach, and we could—"

"I hate the beach."

"No one hates the beach. That's a myth."

With the still-fading seven-inch scar wrapping around her lower leg, a bathing suit was definitely out of the question this year. Maybe forever. "I do. And that's not the point."

"Then let me come with you to Scotland. I'll buy the ticket. You don't even have to—"

Emma shook her head. "I have to do this alone."

She had to prove to herself that what had happened really *had* happened. She remembered all of it, but not the way one might recall a dream. Dreams faded, slipped away. Her time with him was vivid. Alive. She'd found the Montrose estate online, saw pictures of the moor he'd taken her to. She could still almost smell the sweet heather there. If she could just see it, prove it to herself, then, she told herself that would be enough. She would never get Connor back, but she wouldn't completely lose him, either. Then maybe she could move on. She'd shared very little of what she'd been through in the in-between with anyone for lots of reasons. But mostly because, even to her, it sounded crazy. Impossible. And yet...

Emma had looked for him everywhere, hoping. On rooftops, in shadows, in her dreams. But he was nowhere to be found. She hadn't spoken his name. Not once. Perhaps because saying his name out loud would prove she'd crossed over some threshold of crazy. She didn't want Aubrey to look at her that way or say her head injury was to blame. While Emma had struggled through some short-term memory issues, her memory of what had happened in the in-between was crystal clear.

In the hospital, she'd asked a nurse named Cordell if his patients had ever had strange experiences while in comas. He'd admitted he'd had many patients who had, and he'd told her stories that sounded ridiculously plausible to Emma now, though each and every story had been met with some sort of patronizing doubt from loved ones. Cordell said he, for one, believed those stories. He'd heard too many to discredit them with a shrug and a wink. When he'd asked if Emma had experienced something, she'd just nodded. But she didn't want to share about Connor or Violet or about Enoch or Henry or Marguerite. It felt too personal. Too raw. And she could barely think about any of them without crying.

Picking up Winston, who was winding himself around her ankles, she snuggled his furry neck, draping him over her shoulder as he purred. He'd been her comfort in the months she'd been recuperating. He was the only one in the room who could confirm Connor existed. Emma comforted herself now by knowing that Connor must have finally reached his goal. He was, no doubt, finally sitting on his Council and probably happy as a clam now that he'd gotten her and Violet out of his system.

It would, apparently, take her considerably longer.

Her brush with mortality had taken its own toll on her. She'd fought hard to recover her own bravery in the aftermath of the accident. It had been surprisingly hard. She had changed. In some ways, she was stronger than she'd ever been, but in others, she was more vulnerable. And perhaps that was a good thing. Today, she took nothing for granted. What you thought you had your hands around could slip through your fingers in a moment. After this trip, she was determined to push forward with her life and appreciate every day as the gift she knew it was.

"What about Aaron?" Aubrey asked her, pulling her from her thoughts.

"Aaron? What about him?" He'd visited several times, and they had renewed their long friendship. But friendship was all there would ever be between them.

"You know he's interested. I bet he'd go with you to Scotland. If it wasn't for him, we might never have figured out it was Kinsey behind the wheel of that car. Besides, he's crazy about you, Em. I can see it in the way he looks at you every time he's in town."

"I do love Aaron," Emma admitted. "But he's not the one."

Aubrey chugged a sip of wine and bent to pull the salad she'd made from the fridge. "You say that like there's somebody else in the running." She raised her head. "*Is there?*"

Emma felt her cheeks heat. As if he were here in the room with her, she imagined him lounging against a doorway with that annoyingly devastating smile of his that still made her knees go weak. *No. No there's no one else in the running.*

Aubrey straightened. "There is! Ooh, is it Manly? He is super adorable. And now that you're all finished with PT, it would be totally cool to date him. Wouldn't it?"

Emma laughed and shook her head. "Manly" was Aubrey's secret code name for Michael—her very well-built, gorgeous physical therapist—a name often followed by the phrase *please date him*. But Emma had already met Michael's significant other, Benjamin. So that was a hard no.

"Stop. Please. I'm not dating Michael or Aaron or anyone now. I'm just going to do me for a while. If there's one thing I've learned out of all this, it's that life goes by too fast. And I haven't been living it the way I need to. I've been married to my job. You said so yourself. So, this trip is the start to something new. I want to go, and I'm going. And I'm not taking any man with me."

"I never said you were married to your—" Aubrey blinked, apparently remembering that she, in fact, had. "At least I never said that to you."

True, she'd said it to the detective. Supposedly out of her hearing. "Never mind. The point is, I'm not the same old Emma I used to be. You're just all going to have to get used to the new me."

Jacob breezed in through the front door from work without knocking, which had become his custom since he practically lived here now that he and Aubrey were engaged. "I like the new you. What are we talking about?" He dropped his briefcase by the door.

Aubrey kissed him at the end of the island and poured him a glass of wine. "We're talking about Emma 2.0, who's having a software glitch regarding a certain solo Scotland trip."

He shrugged. "Well, I think it's a great idea. You go,

Emma. You deserve a vacation after everything. Enjoy."

"Thank you, Jacob. You're my favorite nearly nephew."

"Traitor," Aubrey mumbled.

Jacob kissed Emma on the cheek and took a sip of wine. "Hey, guess who called me today?" The girls were all ears. "The Smithsonian."

That little green piece of glass in Lizzy's peace necklace, the one no one could explain ending up in her hand in the hospital room? Turned out it wasn't glass at all but an actual emerald. A huge, rare emerald, cut in a very rare way. After they'd gotten over the shock of that revelation, the jeweler who'd assessed it suggested sending it to someone who knew more about rare stones than he did.

"And?" Aubrey asked.

Jacob grinned. "Are you ready for this? According to the museum, our emerald was one your mom and dad must have found in that shipwreck off the Florida coast that was reputed to carry bounty from rebels in Spain from the early seventeen hundreds."

"*What?*" they gasped in unison.

"That stone once sat in the crown of the young Maria Luisa of Savoy, queen to King Phillip the Fifth, of Spain. That crown was stolen some three hundred years ago, during the War of the Spanish Succession, along with dozens other jewels and gold that belonged to the queen and the Spanish king."

"So," Aubrey said, "what happened to the rest?"

"The crown and the other jewels were returned to the Spanish government 'anonymously,' except for that one stone. The one you have. The Smithsonian was the facilitator in that donation. While they couldn't legally divulge the names of the donors, I asked Dr. Covey to cough twice if I said the names of those responsible—Lizzy and Daniel—and he coughed twice. They believed and were told by this 'anonymous' source that the stone you have was never recovered."

Shocked, Aubrey set her wine down, carefully staring at the glass. "Then we have to return it. It doesn't belong to me. It belongs to Spain and her history. It belongs in that crown with all the rest."

Emma took a gulp of her wine. "Your mom wanted you to have something from her. Legally, it was hers to do with what she wanted. It was her last gift to you. It must be worth a fortune, Aubrey."

She poured salad dressing onto the salad and tossed it. "I know. It was my birthstone and hers, and that's probably true. But I can't keep it now that I know. And selling it back to Spain feels wrong." She met Emma's gaze. "So, no. I'll donate it in my parents' name—on the condition that the whole discovery and donation is finally credited to them from Spain's end. At least then they'll be remembered. They'll make history."

Jacob kissed her cheek. "Then that's what we'll do."

Aubrey blinked back the emotion that filled her eyes and

lifted the bowl. "Great. Now who wants salad?"

THIRTY-SIX HOURS LATER, Emma exited a taxi at the front entrance to the Montrose estate, a grand old mansion covered on one wall with ivy and moss. The drive from Glasgow had been long and exhausting after a very long flight from the West Coast. But worth it, she decided, staring at the sweeping gravel-lined driveway that led to the home. The stone crunched under the wheels of the taxi as it drove away, leaving her standing alone in the courtyard of the three-hundred-year-old mansion beside her suitcase.

Built around a courtyard complete with a turret with a Scottish flag waving overhead, the restoration-style estate was built completely of finely cut fieldstone and looked as much a part of the local landscape as the wild heather carpeting the moors above it. Wind-carved trees edged the property that sat near the ocean cliffs, and a formal garden that looked not nearly as grand as it must once have been filled the center of the courtyard.

Emma closed her eyes, imagining Connor walking here as a boy and as a young man with Violet, who'd met him here on this very spot. A deep sense of déjà vu washed over her. This was not only the house she'd seen from the hillside with Connor in the in-between but it was the place Violet had known centuries earlier, the place where she'd fallen in love with the same man Emma had.

She hadn't believed any of that to be possible before her accident. But so much of who she'd once been was different now. If Gran were still here, she'd tell her about this place. All about the afterlife and the in-between and how she'd fallen in love with an angel. Gran would believe her, even if no one else did.

"Emma James?"

The woman's voice came from behind her, and Emma turned to find a tall, aristocratic woman standing in the massive doorway. Her hair was flaming red, swept up into a messy bun. She looked to be nearly forty, with pale, porcelain skin and red lips. She reached a hand out to Emma as she approached. "Aileen McCormack. We spoke on the phone."

Her brogue was thick, but not so thick that Emma didn't understand her. Not so with the taxi driver who'd had to repeat himself several times when asking where she was heading. Emma took her hand with a smile. "Yes. I'm Emma."

"Welcome to the Montrose House. Is that all ye came with?" she asked, indicating her small bag.

"Yes. I'm not here for long. I like to travel light these days."

"Well, come in and I'll show ye to your room. And then we can have a look 'round if ye'd like. There's a lot to see here."

"I'd like that."

The house was grander inside than out, with wood paneling everywhere and huge oil paintings and portraits hanging on every wall. Three hundred years of history was on these walls. Most of the furniture looked like it had been here for nearly as long. Everything looked fresh, though, renovated for modern times, and there was a warm fire burning in the enormous fireplace in the main hall.

"It's lovely," she said as Aileen walked her up the curved staircase to the second floor. "I'm not sure what I expected."

"Most of what ye see here has been preserved over the centuries and well looked after. Of course, we've made improvements, like electrical and heating, but except for the more modern furniture in the library, where lounging is encouraged, most of the furniture is period accurate and some has been with the estate for at least two hundred years. This estate was actually the second family home of the first duke of Montrose, the first residence bein' in Glasgow, but much of their time was spent right here even as the duke was away on business."

The second home? Emma shook her head, unable to wrap her mind around that kind of wealth. Her room was at the top of the stairs, a huge room with brocaded wallpaper in shades of burgundy. A four-poster cherry wood bed sat against one wall opposite the fireplace that already had a fire crackling in it.

"This is our off-season," Aileen explained. "It's a bridal

suite usually, but no one's using it now, so lucky you!"

"Gorgeous. Do you do many weddings here?"

"All the time. It's verra romantic, don't you agree? We're generally booked up during summers, but o' course that's when the heather's bloomin' up the hill. Makes for beautiful wedding photos."

Emma looked out the window. It overlooked the ocean, not the hillside, and the sea looked gray and unsettled today. "You must love working in a place like this."

"Aye, I work here, but my husband and I, we actually own it."

"Oh, I didn't realize the estate had left the family."

"*Och*," she said, straightening out a wrinkle of the duvet cover on the bed. "It didna."

"But your name is McCormick—?"

"That's my husband's name. No, my father was a Montrose in a long line of 'em, and I'm the only child. So, here we are."

Emma blinked. She was standing here talking with a direct relative of Connor's. But how? Who in that family had ended up having children?

Aileen fussed with a curtain, opening it a little wider. "Like many estates such as ours, we've had our struggles since the early part of the last century to keep up with this old place. Times bein' what they are, many are selling off the old estates to big business only to be torn down and replaced with modern buildings and even corporate business parks, if ye can believe it. But we couldn't see our way clear to do that to this old dame. She's dear to us. And dear to the history of our family."

They toured the house together, and Aileen showed her the many rooms of the once grand family. The music room, complete with a grand piano, and the parlor. A nursery that was still in use for guests. The kitchen was modernized, fit for a chef, but a piece of it had been left as it was, looking more like a scene from *Downton Abbey* than the rest of the kitchen. "So many wonder what it was like, d'ye ken?" Aileen said.

Above the fireplace in the library was a portrait that stopped Emma in her tracks. She made a sound. Not quite a gasp, but then again perhaps it was.

"*Och*. Aye, that there was the third duke of Montrose, circa 1801, named Connor Montrose. Quite a handsome bit, eh? Looks like he might just step out of that painting, doesn't he? Must've made hearts flutter in his day. Pity was his life was short and saw a tragic end, but I'll share a bit more on that later in the tour."

Emma could only stare at the painted portrait, which was larger than life but a remarkable likeness in its way of the Connor she knew, down to the twinkle of mischief in his beautiful eyes. She already knew the ending to his story, but to see him here, in the home he'd loved, still imbuing the place with his warmth…it made her heart ache all over again.

Outside, the stables remained intact, with a few horses

belonging to Aileen and her husband, Evan, lazing in the fragrant straw-strewn stalls. Emma rubbed the velvety nose of the chestnut gelding who poked his head out to say hello.

"We still keep some sheep on the property, too, though I myself don't know the first thing about them, other than they keep our lawns trimmed. We have a shepherd who watches over them. And these two allow us to ride them now and then. Lazy chaps. But we love them. And I've got a fancy coop behind the house with chickens who give us fresh eggs every morning for your breakfast. If it's history you're wantin,' if ye look right up there by those cliffs," Aileen went on, looking out through the barn doors, "close to that large boulder was the infamous site of one of our family's biggest scandals. Or, if you will, our saddest days."

"Of course, you mean Connor Montrose, I assume? The duel?"

Surprise widened Aileen's eyes. "Why, that it is. However did ye know that? It's really buried quite deep in the archives of our history now. Though 'tis a story I like to tell our guests. Gives the place a wee bit of romanticism, d'ye ken?"

"I might know a bit more than a little of your history."

"Really? Then you know of the scandal, of course, with the duke's younger sister, Rowena—my fifth great-grandmother—and how it affected the family."

"Yes. It was a terrible thing that happened to her. So unfair."

"It was. And you must know the young duke's brother, Arthur, became the duke of Montrose shortly after Connor's untimely death. Then he himself died not too long after that. His death was rumored to be quite painful and drawn out, though some claimed he deserved that end for the greedy ne'er-do-well he was. He nearly sank the estate with his gambling. In the end, it was their poor, near-ruined sister, Rowena, to whom the estate came down, and she carried it down to her children. She lived practically as a hermit for years before marrying. Her marriage to a wealthy commoner turned out to be a love match after all. So that all worked out for her.

"But in a shameful twist of fate," she continued, "the very woman the Connor Montrose had been set to marry before his death—"

"Violet?" Emma helpfully supplied.

"Why, yes. It was Violet. Violet Gray. She wound up marrying the man who killed him."

"But not by choice," she said, petting the neck of the horse in the stall nearest her. The horse blew a fragrant, hay-y breath into her hair.

Aileen looked at her sideways. "Oh, I ken it was verra much by choice, dear. She bore him several children before dying in childbirth. She played some dark part in the death of the duke—Connor Montrose—and the scandal that Rowena was caught in as well."

"Aileen," Emma said, pulling a small book from her bag.

"I hope you won't mind, but I've brought something I wanted you to have. I think it belongs with the estate and might just clear up any misunderstandings that linger about Connor Montrose and Violet Gray. In this book are excerpts from a diary. Violet Gray's diary about that time. I've tagged the pages for you."

"Really? But how in the world did you—"

"A friend found it for me in a dusty library. I mean no disrespect by bringing it to you. But I think you'll find that what you were told happened was quite the opposite. And I think the truth is the truth, no matter when it's revealed."

Aileen turned the book over in her hands and flipped open the pages. "Well, I'll certainly give it a look. I can't imagine—But who knows? Perhaps we'll get a better story out of this than the original, d'ye ken?"

"Oh, I ken," Emma said. "I really, really do."

IT TOOK EMMA until the next morning to work up the nerve to hike up to the old ruin above the Montrose estate. She'd slept little the night before, despite the comfortable surroundings and the fire crackling in the fireplace in her room. Instead, she'd found herself wandering down to the main hall to stare at his portrait, hanging there among the others. For a long time, she'd sat listening to the fire crackle in the fireplace, studying the portrait. It almost did him justice but couldn't compete with her memory of the real thing. The likeness didn't quite capture his quiet confidence or the gentleness in his eyes, those times when he'd leaned in to kiss her or tease her or protect her. Or the time he'd rescued Lannie's son, Nathan, from the tree. Instead, the artist had painted a certain arrogance into his expression that didn't fit the man she'd come to know. But that would be her secret.

She'd come to Scotland to prove to herself that what she'd experienced was real. And beyond a shadow of a doubt, she knew now it had been. The portrait of Connor, the story Aileen had told her about his past. She couldn't have known any of it on her own. The book she'd given to Aileen she'd ordered off the internet. It had taken weeks and weeks to arrive. But once she'd held it in her hands, she'd known that Elspeth had been real as well. When she finished here, she intended to visit her in Leyton Grove and thank her. Maybe invite her to lunch. There would be so much to talk about with a woman like her. A woman who knew all about angels.

The air was still chilly, and the hike up the hillside was steeper than she remembered, though probably it was her imperfect leg that made it feel so. She hiked up the incline slowly, through the calf-high heather that was still weeks from blooming again but a purplish blush breathed across the tops of the plants, shimmering in waves in the cool breeze. Now and then, she'd turn to look at the ocean in the distance and catch her breath. This ocean looked so different from her own. Wilder. Unfathomable. Like this place. Like him.

Finally, she reached the summit and the ruin Connor had brought her to last summer. The ancient stones were nearly another year older, still covered with moss on the north side where the sun rarely shone. Slowly, she climbed to where he'd brought her that day, the parapet that overlooked the entire moor.

Pushing aside the overgrown vines and weeds clinging to a wall, she saw what she'd come to see. She brushed away the vegetation around the carved letters there: *VG + CM*. "Violet Gray and Connor Montrose," she whispered.

Emma smiled. Of course it was there. She'd known it would be. Tears gathered behind her eyes, and she willed them back. No use getting emotional. This changed nothing, really. She just felt grateful to have survived what had happened. To have known him, if only for a couple of days. She had nothing to prove to anyone anymore. She knew what she knew and that was all that mattered. Life-changing epiphanies aside, though, it felt completely ironic that just when she'd become ready to allow love in her life, the one man she fell in love with wasn't even human.

Then something caught her eye. She frowned as she got up from the weed-littered walkway and inhaled sharply. There, at eye level, freshly carved in the stone was another set of initials: *CM + EJ*.

"Connor Montrose and Emma James." *How in the world—?*

Her fingers gently traced the deep cuts in the stone. For real now, there was no stopping the tears that ran down her cheeks. "Oh, Connor—" she shouted to the moors. "Just when I'm ready to accept being without you, you have to go and do something dumb like this."

Only the wind answered her, blowing her hair until it whipped across her damp cheeks.

She pulled out her phone and snapped a photo of the initials. Not to show anyone else, but for herself. Her only actual physical proof that she hadn't lost her mind.

But then…she caught sight of someone climbing the hill. Too far away to make out, she could tell it was a man. A man whose walk looked oddly familiar.

Emma's lips parted in shock. It couldn't be. Striding up the moor as if the climb was nothing, he kept coming, head down, moving around rocky barriers and thick stands of Scottish heather.

Willing herself to move, Emma pushed away from the wall and raced down the stone stairs to the bottom of the ruin, where she stood waiting. A thousand thoughts raced through her mind in a giant muddle.

It can't be him. She squinted harder at the approaching figure. *This is what comes of jet lag and then staying up all night staring at his face.*

Maybe I've conjured up this figment of my—

Close your eyes. When you open them, he'll be gone.

Except when she opened her eyes, he was still there. Closer now. Beyond any doubt. It was him, not some figment. She could hear the ragged heave of his breath as he drew nearer. The crunch of his boots against the rocky soil.

Steadying herself against the stones behind her, she backed up as he drew closer, staring up at her with that heart-stopping smile.

"Is it…really you?" she whispered.

"Dinna be afraid, Emma," he said, coming to a breathless stop before her.

But she was. She swallowed hard but stood her ground. He looked…beautiful, perfect…*damp*. His hair was stuck to his forehead, and she reached up hesitantly and gently pushed it back. His skin felt warm. "You're…*sweating*."

"Aye." He wiped his brow with the back of his sleeve—a motion that nearly stopped her heart. "Gravity will take some getting used to."

Still, she could only stare at him. *Some getting used to? What did that mean? Gah!* Her brain wasn't working right!

"Are ye not even a wee bit glad to see me?"

She steepled her hands against her mouth, against the hope that she was wrong. That he hadn't come to take her, this time in the other direction. "That depends."

"On what?"

She swallowed hard. "On whether you're here because I somehow just gave myself a heart attack walking up this hill?"

A relieved laugh escaped him, and he shook his head. "No, *mo ghràdh*. Not this time."

Thank God. "Then why…*how* are you here like this?"

He brushed the backs of his fingers against her cheek, then skimmed them down the length of her arm until he'd threaded his fingers with hers. He brought her hand to his mouth. "I'm here because I couldna be anywhere else. I tried. I did. I went to the Council, the place I'd always thought I wanted to be. But I didna fit in there. Truth is I didna fit in anywhere anymore. Ye ken, there was a piece of me missin'. See, I'd left it behind on my last visit here, and without that, nothin' felt good or right. It just felt like a jagged ache where…where you should be."

Emma finally took a breath. But she couldn't dare hope it was for more than just a moment. "So…you dropped by for a visit?"

"I'm not goin' back, Emma."

"What? You mean—?" She covered his hand with hers. "They let you go?"

"I wasna a prisoner. 'Tis no' like that."

Hope fluttered in her chest. "Then…like Elspeth?"

"Somethin' like that." He pulled her closer until she was pressed up against him. "'Twas a bit more complicated in my case. But 'twas Marguerite's doin' all along to put us together, to fix the tear in our soul circle. To mend what was broken in me."

"Broken?" Emma shook her head. "You weren't broken, Connor. You were only wounded. And wounds heal." She glanced down at her leg. "And when they do, you get back up and start again."

He stared at her for a long moment, taking in the sight

of her. "I want to start again with you, Emma. I canna go back. I'm mortal now. That canna be undone. But I have no right to think ye feel the same fer me as I do fer you. And I wouldna presume to—"

She pressed two fingers against his lips. "Oh, but I really, really wish you would." Then she replaced her fingers with her mouth and kissed him deeply. He was warm and solid and as human as any woman could wish for. They wrapped their arms around each other, and he kissed her back until they both ran out of air. Then he kissed her again. Her insides fluttered like the wings of a trapped bird. She could hardly contain her happiness.

Somehow, this kiss was different from the kisses he'd given her as a celestial. This one was full of hope and possibility, all the things they couldn't have wished for before. Because somehow a miracle had happened. He was here. With her. And they could imagine a future together.

"I love ye, Emma," he whispered against her mouth.

"I love you, too." But she had to ask. "Just checking. You're sure it's me and not Violet you love? Because I can never be—"

"Violet is my past, and as sure as I'm standin' here in your arms, yer my future." His fingers splayed against her back. "'Tis you, Emma. 'Twill always be you that owns my heart."

That was all she needed to hear. She swayed against him and smiled against his mouth. "All this time, I was sure I'd never see you again."

"Ye couldna see me, *mo ghràdh*, but I was watchin' you. Watchin' you heal and fight to get your life back. And all I could think was…*I'm in the wrong place.* Ye inspired me to fight fer myself. Fer what I knew we should be."

We. She liked the sound of that word. The cool wind scoured across the moor, whipping around them like an embrace. "What does that mean? *Mo ghràdh.*"

He gave a little shiver of desire as her mouth caressed his ear. "It means 'my love.' Which is what ye are."

"*Mo ghràdh,*" she repeated, smiling against his mouth now. "Promise you'll always call me that."

"I swear."

"Tsk. Angels can't swear," she teased, pressing a finger against his mouth.

He caught her finger between his teeth, then kissed it. "Then 'tis a good thing I'm not one anymore, as I'm greatly lookin' forward to bein' fully mortal again, ye ken?"

Emma blushed. "Oh, I do, indeed. But how will I ever explain you to everyone? That I just picked up this handsome Scot on my short trip here and brought him home with me?"

He smiled. "Just tell them ye met me where the earth and the sky meet, at the edge of Scotland, where all good things begin."

She laughed. "Hmmm. Why didn't I think of that?"

"Ye'll come 'round. I'll make a true Scotswoman of ye yet."

They started down the hill together holding hands. All

around them, the tiny branches of heather imparted their mossy scent as their legs brushed them. And beyond, the sea stretched out to the horizon.

"I'll need to call you something else. At least for the time being."

"Why is that?"

"I can't introduce you to Aileen as Connor Montrose. She'd…well, she'd faint."

"Who's Aileen?"

"Oh," she said, "just your great-great-great-great niece."

"My—*Och*. Now I feel old. Well, I ken ye can just call me Farm Boy." He winked at her.

"No. I called you that before I really knew you. How about Westley?"

"Westley, eh? The brave, strong, and loyal one?"

"Don't forget helpful."

"Right. Does that make you the princess, then?"

She tucked her arm around his and leaned against his shoulder. "Oh, yes, without a doubt, *mo ghràdh*. Without a doubt in the world."

The End

Want more? Check out Elspeth and Sam's story in *The Christmas Fix Up*!

Join Tule Publishing's newsletter for more great reads and weekly deals!

If you enjoyed *Calling All Angels,*
you'll love the other books in…

The Guardian Angel Chronicles series

Book 1: *Every Time a Bell Rings*

Book 2: *The Christmas Fix Up*

Book 3: *Calling All Angels*

Available now at your favorite online retailer!

More books by Barbara Ankrum

The Canadays of Montana series

The Canaday clan is like so many modern families today: blended, flawed and full of love for each other. The series follows the Canaday sisters—Olivia, Kate and Eve—strong yet vulnerable women who have careers and challenges that most of us face as they search for balance in their lives. As is also so often true, their strengths are also their weaknesses when it comes to finding and recognizing true love when it knocks on their door.

Book 1: *A Cowboy to Remember*

Book 2: *Choose Me, Cowboy*

Book 3: *Holiday Hearts*

Book 4: *A Cowboy to Keep*

Band of Brothers series

For the five ex-warrior Navy SEALs who call themselves the Band of Brothers, honor and loyalty are a way of life. But so is the damage each of them faces in the aftermath of the war. They've conquered the physical challenges of the battlefield, but now their struggle is to heal their souls and begin again. Despite the unwavering support of their brothers, each must navigate his own way toward that new beginning. And finding love might just be the key to everything.

Book 1: *Unsung Hero*

Book 2: *Once a Hero*

Book 3: *Unexpected Hero*

Available now at your favorite online retailer!

About the Author

Barbara Ankrum has a thing for the West and has written both historical and contemporary romances, all set in that magical place. Twice nominated for RWA's RITA Award, her bestselling books are emotional, sexy rides with a touch of humor. Barbara's married and raised two children in Southern California, which, in her mind, makes her a native Westerner.

Thank you for reading

Calling All Angels

If you enjoyed this book, you can find more from all our great authors at TulePublishing.com, or from your favorite online retailer.

TULE
PUBLISHING

Made in the USA
Monee, IL
17 October 2022

16052494R00143